"I'm usually very good at restraint," Gio told her truthfully. "But right now, right here with you…I'm not feeling it, *cara.*"

His boldness made Leah feel outrageously shy and she could feel her skin heating and tightening over her bones.

"You blush," he said in apparent wonderment.

"Occasionally—"

"Will you blush if I ask you to come upstairs with me?"

"P-probably," Leah muttered as he pushed away his untouched coffee and stood up to extend a hand to her.

Her heart began to pound inside her as she too got up and reached for that hand, feeling rather like a drowning swimmer and fighting all her insecure feelings to the last ditch. This raw, powerful sense of connection was something new and different for her, but she would get used to it, being very adaptable as she'd had to be throughout her life, she told herself firmly.

The Stefanos Legacy

The billionaire's vow to reunite his family!

When his father dies, renowned Greek tycoon Aristaeus Stefanos is devastated. Not only at the loss of his beloved father, but also the shocking discovery that his father had feet of clay—in the form of two secret daughters!

Ari will do anything to track down his half sisters and offer them his protection—his sense of honor demands nothing less. But his priorities are turned upside down when it's revealed he also has an orphaned baby niece. Ari must put his quest to find his long-lost family on hold to focus on the tiny infant who needs him—and on finding the bride he needs to claim his niece!

Read Ari and Cleo's story in
Promoted to the Greek's Wife

Read Giovanni and Leah's story in
The Heirs His Housekeeper Carried

Look out for the final book in *USA TODAY* bestselling author Lynne Graham's trilogy, coming soon!

Lynne Graham

THE HEIRS HIS
HOUSEKEEPER CARRIED

Recycling programs
for this product may
not exist in your area.

ISBN-13: 978-1-335-56964-6

The Heirs His Housekeeper Carried

Copyright © 2022 by Lynne Graham

Harlequin Enterprises ULC
22 Adelaide St. West, 41st Floor
Toronto, Ontario M5H 4E3, Canada
www.Harlequin.com

Printed in U.S.A.

Lynne Graham was born in Northern Ireland and has been a keen romance reader since her teens. She is very happily married to an understanding husband who has learned to cook since she started to write! Her five children keep her on her toes. She has a very large dog who knocks everything over, a very small terrier who barks a lot and two cats. When time allows, Lynne is a keen gardener.

Visit the Author Profile page
at Harlequin.com for more titles.

CHAPTER ONE

'THANK YOU…IT'S AMAZING,' Zoe purred with satisfaction, having chosen the flashiest bracelet on offer and holding it up to catch the sunshine filtering through the limo window. 'I *so* deserve this. Diamonds truly are the perfect foil for my beauty.'

A famous supermodel, Zoe had locked her avid and triumphant gaze to the sparkling gems as if she had won the lottery. As Gio had yet to see Zoe show that much appreciation for anything else, that glimpse of entitled avarice and unashamed vanity made his shapely mouth compress. He was glad that their affair was over, the diamonds his final gift.

Greed was a turn-off, a major turn-off for Giovanni Zanetti, and yet the richer he became, the more cunning rapacity he recognised in the women he met. For the very first time in his life he wondered what it would be like to be Mr Nobody from Nowhere, rather than the billionaire owner of a technology empire with a much-envied lifestyle. Until that moment he hadn't known that he could even picture such a fanciful and absurd possibility because he had not appreciated that he had that much imagination. Would women even want him without the diamonds and all the other extravagant trappings he provided? It was an interesting question.

Gio was, first and foremost, a self-made man, who had grown up in dire poverty and deprivation with a violent drug-dealing father and a beaten, uninterested mother. His meteoric rise to phenomenal success had been marred by only one mistake: at twenty-one: he had been conned into marriage by a gold-digger. Aside of that damaging error of judgement, he had, eight years later, already attained almost everything he wanted in life.

Only one major goal had so far eluded him, he acknowledged wryly, and that was the acquisition of his late mother's former familial home, the Castello Zanetti. When his unfortunate *mamma* had shamed her snobbish family by falling pregnant by the local bad boy, they had thrown her out and sold up, moving away to escape the humiliation of the resulting scandal. Although his mama had been a decidedly imperfect parent, alongside his papa, something visceral in Gio had always longed for a connection that rooted him in another world. And the world of history and ancestors that his mother had run from, a family tree that he could proudly claim a connection to as opposed to the shameful one he had been born into with his parents, had enormous pull with him. That house, that family property, meant a great deal to him.

As Zoe trailed a sensual hand of promise down over Gio's lean muscular thigh, he tensed with distaste at the inevitable suspicion that his generous gift had *bought* her sexual enthusiasm. Revulsion gripped him. Shifting away, he was relieved that their association was at an end. Exposed as the vain and mercenary woman she was, the model had lost much of her appeal.

At the same time, Gio was, however, uneasily accustomed to the keen interest that his spectacular good looks invariably invoked. He had not a shred of vanity on that score. Indeed, he actively despised the familiar image that met him in the mirror because it reminded him sickeningly of his brutal, toxic father. The lustrous black hair, the hard chiselled jawline, the classic nose and exotic high cheekbones teamed with unusual ice-blue eyes turned the heads of both men and women in the street.

That same night at a Manhattan party, when he was literally ringed by a circle of beautiful women vying for his attention, Fabian, one of Gio's friends, rolled his eyes to say, 'You have got it made. Any woman you want whenever, however. I don't think you appreciate just how lucky you are.'

'If I weren't rich and single, I wouldn't be half as appealing,' Gio retorted with innate cynicism and an acute sense of boredom.

He thought instead of the magnificent freedom of walking the beach at his rarely used house in Norfolk, England, of the cool refreshing breeze and the isolation there. He needed a break. That awareness in mind, he checked the time in the UK before calling the caretaker to instruct her to set the house up for his arrival the coming weekend.

In an anxious tone of apology and audible dismay at his unforeseen request, Miss Jenkins confided that she had broken her ankle and would need to find someone else to ensure that the coastal mansion was prepared for his occupation. Apologising for the short notice he was giving her, Gio voiced his sympathy and immediately offered a substantial amount of extra cash that the older woman could use to persuade someone trustworthy to take on that necessary task and get it done in time.

As always, he mowed down any hint of opposition like a steamroller that simply refused to be redirected. Life since adulthood had made Gio highly unfamiliar with disappointment, and even a disturbing hint of that possibility was sufficient to make him more determined than ever to leave the business world and designing women behind for a few days and enjoy that energising breeze...

Leah tempted Spike out from behind the chair. 'Come on...the vet's gone home. You don't need to be nervous because you've had all your treatment now,' she murmured soothingly.

A scruffy three-legged Yorkshire terrier with an incongruous purple bow on top of his tufty head crept into view. He was exceedingly small and very scared. He was terrified of all men, even of the kindly vet, but that didn't stop him from trying to sneak up behind unsuspecting males and nip them in the back of the leg. Luckily for his victims, Spike had few remaining teeth after years of neglect. As he surged into her arms, she lifted him to pet him while she absently listened to the conversation her former foster mother, Sally, was having on the phone with her sister, Pam Jenkins.

'Absolutely *silly* money,' Sally was proclaiming, her round good-natured face below her halo of grey curls full of incredulity. 'Clearly, the man has more money than sense, but Leah can do it, of course she can. A bit of shopping, a bit of cleaning, a few beds to make up...not a problem, Pam. Will you *please* stop worrying about it now? Of course, the man's not going to sack you just because you broke your ankle!'

Sally came off the phone. 'The Gazillionaire is coming...'

Leah grinned at the announcement, sitting back on her heels, a cascade of glossy dark ringlets framing her oval face and then tumbling back across her shoulders, her big brown eyes dancing. 'So I gathered...and I assume that I'm going to carry out Pam's usual work for her—'

'Yes, she's got a shopping list that he forwarded to her, says it's the usual fancy stuff you'll have to go into town to find. My goodness, do you realise what this means?' Sally carolled in excitement. 'You will actually get to *see* inside Shore House!'

The buyer of the imposing building had been

christened 'the Gazillionaire' once word of the wildly expensive restoration and improvements he had ordered had filtered out into the nearby village. Curiosity had raged about the new owner and the house but, over the three years that the Italian had owned it, he had made very infrequent visits and neither he nor any of his guests had ever ventured into the village and even Pam had never actually met him in the flesh. Apparently, he travelled with his own personal household staff. A landscape firm in Norwich looked after the grounds and the indoor pool. Sally's sister, Pam, was the caretaker and cleaner, but she had never dared to bring anyone with her on her visits because the house was full of cameras and she didn't want to break the rules and lose her job. For the same reason she had been afraid to take any photos of the property.

'I'll go and get changed,' Leah proffered, because she was still in her pyjamas. 'When do you need me to go over there?'

'Asap. So, Pam's lawn and *her* shopping will wait,' Sally told her because, with Sally busy running her small animal shelter, Leah had been looking after Pam while she recuperated from her fall. The two older women were close but, even though there was space in Sally's old

farmhouse, her younger, single sister had preferred to remain in her village home, pointing
out cheerfully that she and Sally squabbled
when they got under each other's feet.

'My goodness, I just said that you would
take care of the Gazillionaire's house for Pam
without even first asking you if you would!'
Sally suddenly exclaimed in belated apology.
'What on earth was I thinking of? With your
fancy degree, cleaning would be far too much
of a comedown for you—'

'Of course, I'll do it…aren't I living here
free of charge? And don't talk nonsense. I'll
do virtually anything to earn cash right now,'
Leah admitted without embarrassment. 'I hope
it *is* absolutely silly money I'll be paid too. You
could do with some of it for the shelter. That
last vet bill was steep.'

'I don't want the money!' Sally informed
her sternly. 'Look at all the help you've given
Pam. You've kept her garden, taken her to the
hospital and done her shopping when I've been
too busy—'

'You took me in when I had nowhere else
to go and I'm grateful, so let's not hear any
more about cleaning being beneath me,' Leah
urged, thinking that cleaning was no more
humble than stacking shelves in the village

supermarket, which she had also done. Unfortunately, there were few local employment opportunities. Her business degree was no more use where she lived than it had proven to be in London where, only two years earlier, she had embarked on what she initially hoped would eventually become a successful career. As her mind threatened to linger on everything that had gone so terribly wrong in the city, she buried the thought, because there was nothing attractive about bitterness.

Leah had learned very young that life could contain many bad moments, a great deal of loss and frequent disappointments, but she had taught herself not to dwell too long on the negatives. There had been Oliver, who had broken her heart, but before he came along she had lost her father, then her mother and her two siblings, and whenever she thought about her missing family a terrible wave of sadness would threaten to engulf her. Her mother was dead, and it was hard to care about whether or not her father was dead or alive because he had chosen his *other* family over his family with her mother, making it clear that she and her siblings were second best.

Eventually, however, Leah hoped to trace and get back in touch with her twin brother and younger sister, but that was likely to take both patience and money. She had seen her brother several times over the years, but their relationship had been strained by his drug addiction and his willingness to steal from her to fund it.

Sadly, she had left London with nothing but credit-card debt, which she had only recently contrived to pay off. Before she could move out of Sally's home and return to urban living, she would have to have a nest egg saved up to cover accommodation and at least the chance of a proper job.

An hour later, Leah was scouring the supermarket and eventually a delicatessen for the more unusual ingredients on the shopping list. Wakame seaweed and Thai basil were not easily found in a small rural town. Equivalents or total substitutes purchased with the credit card Pam had entrusted her with, Leah drove to Shore House.

A long winding driveway led to the grey stone house, bookmarked with a substantial round tower at either end and embellished with a forest of tall elaborate chimneys and equally tall mullioned windows. Built in the style of Victorian Gothic, it was a white elephant of a house, which had been fortunate to find a buyer. Its biggest selling point, though, was its

multiple views of the sea and the long sandy
shoreline that lay only yards below the edge
of the gardens. Parking in the cobbled courtyard and gathering up the shopping, Leah let
herself in the back door, punched in the code
for the alarm and headed inside.

Cameras high up the walls silently swivelled as she moved, making her inordinately
conscious of their presence. She put the shopping away first in the vast kitchen with its huge
central island, granite worktops and top-of-
the-range fancy stove. Pam had written down
explicit instructions about where to find everything she needed. Armed with the com-
prehensive cleaning box stored in the pantry,
Leah went upstairs to start her work. The foyer
was a breathtaking space, the very centre of
which was the split staircase, which went up
one flight and then divided imposingly into
two. All that ornately carved wood would be
a challenge to dust, she acknowledged ruefully
as Spike scampered at her heels.

According to Pam, the six principal bedrooms were routinely prepared for guests and
that was where Leah began, dusting and vacu-
uming as she went before shaking out the expensive linens and deftly making up the beds.
The property might be Victorian, but the fur-

nishings were light and contemporary, using the elaborate carving and fancy plasterwork as an ornamental backdrop, rather than allowing it to dictate the whole mood. Surprisingly, that decorative approach worked, and Leah was eager to explore the whole house. Unfortunately, she knew she would have her work cut out just to cover the basics of cleaning such a large property and she didn't have time to dawdle. Despite regular sips from her water bottle, Leah got steadily warmer even though she was only wearing denim shorts and a tee.

Having completed the bedrooms and ignored the dusty staircase altogether because it looked as though it would take hours, Leah explored the ground floor, choosing where she would concentrate her energies next while reminding herself that she would be able to return to clean again the next day. Hopefully nobody would arrive before the following evening, or her goose would be cooked because no way was she likely to get around the whole house before then! It was simply too big.

Closing the door firmly on a library that was a tremendous temptation to a book lover, Leah embarked on the vast sitting room instead, relieved that the house was gloriously empty of the kind of knick-knacks that her foster mother and her sister adored. There was art on the walls and occasional elegant sculptures but no clutter to lift or work around.

She was contemplating cleaning the kitchen when she saw a door at the end of the ground-floor corridor that had previously escaped her notice. She sighed, already tired and hot as she was and wincing at the awareness that she would be returning at the crack of dawn the next morning to complete the cleaning. She had been cutting corners, she conceded guilt-ily, the undusted stairs looming like a mon-ster in the back of her brain as she cleaned the cloakroom. And what about the dining room, the smaller sitting room, the library and the room with the giant snooker table?

Before she tackled the kitchen she decided to explore through that closed door, lest it was concealing a whole host of other rooms that would require her attention. The door took her into a tiled hall and she crossed it to move through glass double doors into the indoor pool area, which she had totally forgotten about. Off to one side and entirely separate there was a gym, and on the other side there was a very fancy Victorian circular conserva-tory area packed with towering tropical plants kept healthy by a temperature-controlled environment.

In front of her, however, stealing centre stage, was a curved, arched and tiled wall that housed an extraordinary lotus-shaped fountain fanning water down into the swimming pool. High above, an ornate cupola and a ring of gorgeous stained-glass windows cast a rainbow of light down onto the shimmering surface. Mermaids were entwined in a huge, tiled panel above the fountain. It was very Victorian and very exotic, and it had been so beautifully restored that it might have been built the day before. Presumably the feature was listed and protected by law, Leah assumed, finding it hard to credit that the Gazillionaire might have conserved the mermaids and the ornate pool out of the goodness of his heart.

Hot and sticky, Leah looked down at the cool water lapping the edge of the tiled steps and sighed with longing. She would strip off and have a sneaky swim *after* she had finished the kitchen, she promised herself. She had no swimsuit, but she could use the clean T-shirt in her bag…or she could swim naked. After all, there was nobody around to see her…

Shaking her head at that amusing thought, Leah walked back out of the pool area and got stuck in the kitchen, which, all credit to Pam's efforts, required little attention. The pale floor, however, was a different story and she began returning it to pristine perfection. In the aftermath, hot and sweaty from her efforts, she raced upstairs to the cavernous hot press, extracted a big towel from one of the towering fleecy piles and headed straight back down to the pool. It was the work of a moment to undress and walk naked into the water, and that wonderful coolness on her overheated skin was an immediate reward that made her sigh in blissful relief.

Gio walked through the hall, noting the abandoned cleaning box, and he suppressed a sigh as he strode upstairs. The cleaner was still here, which was hardly surprising when he had arrived earlier than he had expected. He, however, wanted the house to himself. He would tell the cleaner to come back tomorrow to finish. He peeled off his jacket, removed his tie and was about to embark on his trousers when he thought he felt something nip at the back of his leg. He swung round but there was nothing there, only a faint suspicion of movement from the throw draped across the foot of the bed. Gio bent down and peered under the bed.

A small, frightened yelp sounded and something brown shot out from below and pelted full speed for the door. It was the size of a rat, but rats didn't have purple bows in their hair so it had to be a dog. The cleaner had brought a dog in with her. Gio frowned, thinking that his dogs in Italy would have made a snack of the wretched little creature. He cast aside his jacket and started back down the stairs again. For the first time he noticed that the door to the pool complex was ajar and he strode down the corridor towards it.

From the doorway he was able to see that he had a naked mermaid in his pool. A mermaid with a topknot of cascading black curls and a pale pink bottom as ripe as a peach showing through the water as she swam. Gio grinned, amused but annoyed because, instead of reacting with the humour he was struggling to restrain, the onus was now on him to play the censorious boss and lay down the law, spelling out what she had done wrong and why she shouldn't be doing it.

'Hi…' Gio murmured quietly, staying well back from the side of the pool, not wishing to make the naked intruder feel threatened.

'Oh, for crying out loud!' the mermaid exclaimed, throwing her hands high in dismay and then lurching across the water to grip the rail at the side to anchor herself. He caught a wickedly alluring flash of full perky breasts adorned with taut brown nipples. 'Who are you? What are you doing here?'

'I think those are my questions to ask,' Gio countered lazily.

Leah tilted her chin. 'I'm here because I'm cleaning the house—'

Gio elevated an ebony brow in measured challenge. 'From the pool?'

An angry flush mantled Leah's cheeks. 'I've been working here all day and I got really hot. The only person that has the right to question me is the owner of this place…and I know that's not you—'

Gio could not help grinning because she kept on coming back at him, refusing to be quelled or cooled. 'And how do you know that? Are you acquainted with the owner?'

'The Gazillionaire?' Leah quipped. 'Are you joking? Of course, I'm not! But I *do* know that you're not him. He looks like a wild mountain man—'

'The Gazillionaire?' Gio queried with raised brows as he repeated that description. 'How…a wild mountain man?'

'I saw a picture of him in a newspaper and

he has long hair and a full beard,' Leah informed him with a rather smug look. 'So, what are you doing here in his house? Are you the gardener?'

'Do I look like a gardener?' Gio asked with interest.

Leah appraised him, which took time because he was very tall and powerfully built. He had cropped black hair and exceptionally light eyes of an unknown hue that were very obvious in his lean bronzed face. He was quite staggeringly good-looking, an acknowledgement that severely unnerved and surprised her and made her wonder why she was still hanging around naked in the water with him present.

'No, you don't look like a gardener,' she admitted uneasily, noting the sunglasses stylishly hooked in the pocket of his red shirt, which was open at the neck. His trousers looked as though they might have been part of a suit, because they were narrow and very fashionable and almost indecently well fitted to his narrow hips and long powerful thighs. He emanated casual sophistication and a distinct urban edginess. 'Not a gardener...you work for the pool company?'

'No,' Gio said quietly.

'Do you work for the mountain man in some other capacity?'

His light eyes danced. 'I might…'

'Well, while you're thinking about that could you move away and turn your back so that I can get out of the water and back into my clothes?'

'I could if I were a gentleman,' Gio told her and shrugged with easy grace. 'I'm not.'

Temper flashed into Leah's caramel-brown eyes. She let go of the rail and swam over to the steps in an attempt to reach for the towel lying at the edge. 'Don't be a pig!' she urged.

Gio laughed with genuine appreciation and scooped up the towel, turning his back and extending it behind him.

The water rippled and shifted noisily, and he imagined her climbing out, close enough to be touched, that pale luscious wet body gleaming with water. She plucked the towel from his grasp and stepped up past him, wrapped from shoulder to calf in the largest towel he had ever seen.

'So, you work for Mr Zanetti,' Leah recapped, dabbing at her damp face with the loose end of the towel. 'Are you a member of his household staff?'

'What do you know about his household

staff?' Gio asked with a frown, wondering what had sparked that incorrect rumour.

'Only that they travel with him, presumably doing his cooking and driving and whatnot—'

'This Gazillionaire sounds pretty helpless,' Gio commented, watching her scoop up her clothes. She was petite rather than tall, but that magnificent head of glossy black curls was spectacular. Add in huge brown eyes, creamy skin, delightful curves and slender shapely legs and she was a remarkably tempting package. Too short for him, of course, because, being six feet five, he preferred taller women and she was a good foot shorter than he was. Only that conviction did not explain why he had got as hard as a rock just looking at her in the towel. She might be small, he conceded, but she was all woman and incredibly sexy.

'He's probably too busy concentrating on the tech stuff that makes the money to waste time doing the ordinary stuff for himself,' Leah contended as she bent to gather up her clothes while wishing that her faded blue undies had not been sitting on top of the pile. 'And maybe he *can't* cook or drive. Not everyone can. I'm a demon behind a steering wheel but I can't cook for peanuts...'

'I'm an excellent cook,' Gio told her, crossing

the floor to yank open a door almost concealed by the tiles. 'Changing facilities in here...'

'Thank you.' Leah gave him a mischievous smile. 'You're more of a gentleman than you think you are.'

'No, I'm not, but being politically correct around women is safer these days,' Gio fired back without hesitation.

Leah vanished into a cubicle where the lights fired up automatically and shed the towel, shivering as she climbed back into her clothes, her bra sticking to her damp flesh as she hurried, thrusting her feet into her battered trainers with a sense of relief. Being naked around a strange man in an empty house was unwise. Who on earth was he? Obviously, he worked for the Gazillionaire in some capacity.

'Are you his cook?' she asked inquisitively as she emerged from the changing area, breathless and flushed.

On the cusp of announcing his true identity, Gio decided on a whim that was seductively playful in comparison to his usual deadly serious state of mind that he didn't want to be a cook any more than he wanted to be himself. 'No, office staff. I'm an executive PA—'

'I was a PA once.'

'How did you end up doing this job?'

'I was a PA for a guy who was hauled away by the police for defrauding thousands of people of their savings. He set up one of those pyramid schemes. He's in prison—'

'Patrick Lundsworth?' Gio incised, mentioning a name that had become a byword for dishonesty and that had been on everybody's lips only months earlier. 'How come you aren't doing time as well?'

'The police questioned me for two days, but I wasn't much use to them. It was my first job out of university and I was the office junior. I made coffee, answered phone calls, checked emails.' Leah grimaced. 'I wasn't in on anything to do with his con. I didn't even meet any of his investors. I was lucky…or so I thought at the time—'

'But you've still ended up cleaning,' Gio reminded her drily, thinking that she was very innocent and confiding for a woman with a stranger.

'Lundsworth has proved to be a very serious blight on my CV. I couldn't get another job in London, so I moved up here to try and get my life sorted,' Leah explained. 'And hopefully memories will eventually fade and I'll be able to get my feet back on the career ladder again.

'Would you like some coffee?' she asked as

she walked away from him. 'I'm taking a break before I get back to work.'

'Not right now. I'm going upstairs to change before I go for a walk on the beach,' Gio responded.

'I'll finish here about six but I'm going to have to come back tomorrow to finish the job,' Leah advanced uncomfortably. 'I hope that will be all right. Is anyone else due to arrive before six tomorrow?'

'No,' Gio confirmed as he headed towards the stairs.

'I'm Leah,' she said quietly. 'What's your name?'

Her easy friendliness made his mouth twist. It had been so long since he had had that from a woman. Women always posed with him and played for a certain effect. It was false and it was fake but, in his world, it was a tried and tested female route to popularity with wealthy men. If he told Leah who he was, she would be aghast, apologising all over the place and out of the house within minutes. And, really, what harm had she done? A dip in his pool? A damp towel?

'I'm Gianni,' Gio told her truthfully, although it was not a diminutive he had used since his mother's death. She had named her son for his father, Giovanni, because she had still been in the first fine flush of love back then and she had called her son Gianni to distinguish between them.

'Have a lovely walk on the beach!' she urged. 'I've got the staircase to tackle.'

Gio smiled. 'Sounds like a challenge.'

'Have you seen how many nooks and crannies are hidden in those carvings?' Leah asked very seriously. 'It's a nightmare.'

Walking along the deserted strand in jeans and a sweater, Gio recalled that conversation and laughed out loud. She would never have acted so normally with him had she known who he really was. 'A wild mountain man'? Could it be that she had seen a photo of him on his return from his charitable trust's trek in Borneo? Afterwards, he had cut his hair shorter and dispensed with the beard he had worn for years. And what was with the Gazillionaire tag? But, *Madre di Cristo*, she was outrageously pretty… *and* currently engaged in cleaning his stairs, he reminded himself wryly.

By the time he returned, she might be gone…although not without the little rat sneakily trailing him along the shore, Gio reckoned, casting a quick eye over his shoulder just in time to see the little dog duck behind a rock to hide. It wasn't the brightest dog he had ever met. It was low to the ground and thought itself invisible behind the rock but, being so tall, Gio could see it clearly, cowering at the risk of being caught. He ignored it. Had it bitten him or tried to bite him earlier in the bedroom? There was no mark on his leg. He smiled, thinking it wasn't much of an attack dog.

An hour later, Gio strode back into the house and found Leah still down on her knees on the stairs, wielding a brush and wiping the woodwork with a cloth. His breath hissed between his even white teeth as he took in the jut of her luscious behind shaped in skin-tight faded denim and he averted his attention, reminding himself that he did not perve over employees... *ever*! Although, strictly speaking, she wasn't working for him, he reflected with a jab of satisfaction. It was stretching a point but when she glanced up at him, her vivid little face framed by that glorious mass of black curly hair and dominated by those huge dark sparkling eyes, whose employee she might be was the very last thing on Gio's mind.

'Stay and join me for dinner,' Gio heard himself urge without any awareness that he had even considered that idea before he spoke.

The immediacy of that random prompting sharply disconcerted him.

Leah flung a startled glance at him and then dropped her head to concentrate on her task. Of course, she would say no, because she had decided six months ago that she was done with men after having wasted a year on a male who had ditched her without a pang. Oliver had been an education and no mistake. He had taught her a lot, hard lessons that had hurt. But didn't cutting herself off from the opposite sex merely hand Oliver yet another victory? A shot of defiance flared inside her at that suspicion.

'OK,' she said casually, as though agreement had not cost her a single moment of consideration. 'I've nothing to rush home for... I assume you're offering to cook?'

A wicked grin slanted Gio's mobile lips as he read her dismay at the prospect that he could be expecting her to whip out the pans. 'Sì...'

'Oh, you're Italian like your boss...that's where your name comes from.' Leah stumbled over that awkward little speech as his pale eyes, the colour of glacier ice, glittered with unhidden amusement. 'Sorry, not very travelled or cosmopolitan here.'

'That has an appeal all of its own,' Gio informed her truthfully, watching her blush, wondering when he had last seen a woman blush around him and quite entranced by it, any doubts he had had about his invitation draining away. He was in the mood for company, he told himself. It was harmless.

In something of a daze, Leah gazed back at him, hopelessly captivated by his looks and charm. She didn't think she had ever come across a more handsome guy unless he had been on a movie screen and even then, in her humble opinion, Gianni could have knocked spots off all competition. He was drop-dead gorgeous and when he smiled, she got butterflies in her tummy as though she were a teenager again. For goodness' sake, she castigated herself, start thinking like a grown-up for once…

CHAPTER TWO

'Do you want a hand?' Leah asked uncertainly from the kitchen doorway.

'You could chop up some of the vegetables if you like,' Gio suggested.

Leah didn't like but Sally had raised her to have manners. Striving not to stare at the male efficiently working with the salmon she had bought at the island unit, she scrubbed her hands at the sink and returned gingerly to the centre of the kitchen. 'Knives over there in the block,' he advised, lifting out another cutting board and settling it on the other side of the unit. 'Could you dice them?'

Leah was sure she could have done had she known what 'dicing' entailed.

Minutes later, Gio watched in silent wonderment as Leah wielded a knife much as though she were sawing up a log for the first time. 'Watch your fingers,' he heard himself say as he strove not to wince or be critical.

'I'm not a child,' she told him drily with an upward glance of her glorious dark eyes just as the knife sliced into a finger, causing her to drop it and yelp in startled pain.

For a split second, Gio said nothing because he was stunned by that level of cooking incompetence, and then he dropped his own knife and went to her rescue. He picked her up like a package and settled her down on one of the bar stools while blood dripped from her and she whimpered, white with shock. 'Let me have a look…no, it won't need stitches,' he informed her soothingly, swiftly registering that she was one of those people terrified by the sight of blood.

White as a sheet, Leah sat shivering on the stool, fighting back the urge to throw up while Gio wrapped the bleeding finger in kitchen towelling to cover it from her gaze. He was incredibly competent in an emergency, she realised dimly as he broke out a first-aid kit and speedily cleaned her up and affixed a plaster to the offending digit.

'There,' Gio completed, pausing only to lift Leah and the stool back to the island unit. 'Now you can watch me cook.'

'I can't possibly—' she began, her throat

tight with embarrassment at the show she had made of herself.

'You can't do anything with your hand out of commission,' Gio countered gently, recognising the glassy sheen of tears in her eyes. 'What's wrong?'

'I was such an idiot. I freaked out at the blood,' she mumbled sickly.

'It affects some people that way,' Gio responded lightly, keen to lighten her mood.

Leah breathed in deep and swallowed so hard that she hurt her throat. 'I was with my mother when she was in an accident and died,' she told him jerkily. 'It's been a problem for me ever since.'

Disconcerted not only by that admission but also by an unfamiliar urge to demand further details about an event that had had such long-lasting consequences for her, Gio pulled a bottle of wine out of the wine cabinet and uncorked it. Such intense curiosity was unlike him, because he didn't tend to get personal with other people lest it encourage them to assume that they could do the same with him. Yet Leah confided in him so easily and he definitely wasn't accustomed to that trait. Was it because he was a stranger? Or was she like that with everybody? Or, even less likely, was she feeling the same weird relaxation in his company that he felt in hers?

'That's not surprising. Don't worry about it,' Gio urged softly, resisting a far too personal prompting to pat her slight shoulder in a comforting motion, utterly unsure whether he liked or disliked the first protective urge any woman since his mother had fired in him.

'But a little cut and suddenly I'm behaving as though I cut my whole hand off…like a drama queen,' Leah framed in severe mortification at that image, which offended her practical soul. 'Sorry about that.'

'It doesn't matter,' Gio dismissed, slotting a glass of red wine into her hand. 'Have a drink and relax.'

Leah breathed again, thinking he was really quite kind and the absolute opposite of her selfish and critical ex-boyfriend, who had been utterly indifferent when her life had fallen apart. Of course, that had likely been because he had neither wanted her nor loved her and she had simply been a useful adjunct to the image he'd chosen to put out in the world. What a gullible, trusting fool she had been with Oliver!

That one glass of wine went to her head a little and she gulped down the water he handed her because she had been getting a bit giggly.

'I'm a cheap date when it comes to alcohol,' she muttered, wondering why on earth she felt that she should always be apologising to him as if she were failing to live up to some perfect ideal.

'I noticed,' Gio murmured, disconcerting her with that piece of frankness. 'I don't want you drinking too much.'

Leah flushed and drank more water in embarrassment rather than inform him that she already knew that one glass of wine was pretty much her limit because Oliver had often mocked her for that weakness.

Gio slid a plate across to her, a plate perfectly adorned with salmon and crisp, colourful vegetables, and she blinked. 'This looks amazing,' she said truthfully. 'When did you start cooking?'

'When I was a student. I like good fresh food and if I wanted to eat it, I had to learn how to make it,' Gio admitted, sinking fluidly down on the stool across from hers and lifting a knife and fork.

'I continued living with my former foster mother while I was a student,' Leah responded. 'And Sally rules her kitchen and would be offended if you tried to cook for yourself, so I was lazy—'

'*Foster* mother?' Gio queried.

'I was in care from the age of eleven. Mum was dead and my father disappeared from our lives when I was a toddler.' Leah lifted and dropped her narrow shoulders. 'Sally became much more than just a foster parent to me. I was lucky.'

'Most people would say you had it tough, rather than lucky,' Gio remarked softly. 'But I know where you're coming from. I didn't have a conventional secure childhood either.'

Her dark eyes widened on his when she thought for a split second that she had glimpsed a world of hurt shadowing his lean strong face and his pale gaze. '*Oh...?*'

But he deflected her curiosity by turning his handsome dark head in the direction of the small dog nervously peering round the edge of the door. 'What's *his* story?'

'Sally runs a small animal sanctuary. Spike was brought in last year. From what we were told he was an older woman's much adored pet until she died in the same accident that lost him his leg. Her partner tied him up in a yard afterwards and neglected him. I think the man beat him as well, maybe for barking or something,' Leah told him in a pained undertone.

'So now he's terrified of men, which is why he won't come in here.'

Gio watched those huge caramel eyes gloss over with compassion and regret on the little animal's behalf and that softness in her, that gentleness he wasn't at all used to seeing in women, seemed to fill him with the most extraordinary lust. As his jeans tightened and his arousal pulsed against his zip, he marvelled at the sheer novelty of her effect on him. It was because she was different, that was all, he reasoned impatiently, an unsurprising reaction when he had clearly become bored with the predictability of the women in his life.

'That's strange, because he followed me all the way along the beach and back. Perhaps I remind him of someone from happier times,' he murmured huskily. 'Would you like coffee?'

That enquiry flustered Leah. Here she was, supposedly cleaning his employer's house, and now *he* seemed to be somehow waiting on her hand and foot and that could only strike her as an uncomfortable development. In haste she slid off the stool to help in some way while he reached for the percolator. For a split second she veered closer to him than she had intended and she froze, her dark gaze utterly entrapped by the pale icy brilliance of his.

His hand settled on her shoulder to steady her as she lurched a little off balance while their eyes kindled and white volcanic heat fired in her pelvis. He lowered his dark head and she waited, full of anticipation, yearning for that connection with every fibre of her being. His wide sculpted mouth brushed hers and she trembled, engulfed in screaming awareness of his proximity. It truly felt like the most exciting thing that had ever happened to her. Her hands lifted of their own volition and closed into his forearms to hold him there and then he kissed her.

And it was every kiss she had never had but always dreamt about: a slow burn of sensation teaching her that her lips and her mouth were a much more sensitive and sensual vehicle than she had ever guessed. The circling caress of his full soft lips on her own made her knees wobble and her heart thump ridiculously fast and when he slid the tip of his tongue into the moist interior of her mouth, she ignited like a burning torch thrown on a bale of hay. She was stunned when every inch of her body responded to that unexpectedly powerful stimulus.

Gio kissed her, her breasts swelled and her nipples snapped taut and her pelvis clenched down deep inside, ensuring that she flushed and shifted her hips in heated awareness like a teenager who had never been kissed before, she acknowledged in mortification. She was shocked by his influence over her, struggling to handle it even while she was mesmerised by the physical feelings engulfing her in pleasure.

Gio lifted his head, so aroused that he almost gritted his teeth at the exuberance of his libido. He didn't know what had come over him, but it was just sex on his terms and therefore an acceptable urge that should not require any greater examination. He stared down at her vibrant little face with intense appreciation gripping him. 'You're beautiful,' he murmured quietly. 'Will you stay here tonight with me?'

A sliver of surprise snaked through Leah at those blunt words, because she had yet to spend the night with *any* man. It galled her to still be untouched at twenty-two years of age, but only a couple of years earlier she had truly believed in saving that ultimate intimacy for a more meaningful relationship. And, most ironically, she had been saving herself for the likes of Oliver, she thought sickly, a man who had never desired her in the first place, although he had tried to pretend otherwise to keep her keen in the girlfriend stakes. Crushingly, that gambit had only worked for him with her *because* she had been naïve and inexperienced with men, and ever since that betrayal she had despised that ignorance of hers, which had left her open and vulnerable to hurt and humiliation.

'Leah…?' Gio prompted in the bottomless silence, wondering what was amiss when her wonderful expressive eyes lowered below her feathery lashes and she evaded his gaze.

'I thought you were making coffee,' Leah reminded him daringly, playing for time, struggling to get her frantic thoughts and those unwelcome memories of her ex under control. 'I'm thinking about your invitation… You're very er…frank—'

'How else would I be? You are single, *aren't* you?' His ebony brows pleated at the sudden realisation that she might not be, that he was in a different place with her than he normally was with women. She hadn't offered herself to him first, hadn't sought his attention, and a bare ring finger meant nothing these days when she might already have children and a partner.

'Yes, free as a bird,' Leah confirmed in a rather brittle response, because Oliver's deception had cruelly wounded her self-respect.

Gio was slightly disconcerted by the surge of relief that immediately assailed him.

Leah tilted her chin up as she slid back up onto the bar stool, deeming herself safer from being stupid with him at that distance because she still didn't know how she had ended up in his arms, only that the temptation to get closer to him had been irresistible and incredibly strong. That she had never felt that way before had impressed her. Life was short, she told herself, and she planned to make the most of it without falling for any more males of Oliver's ilk. 'I'm very loyal,' she told him with quiet pride. 'I wouldn't have kissed you had there been someone else in my life.'

Gio was almost amused by that pointed and pure declaration of loyalty and honesty, which only accentuated the gulf between them. After all, he had never been able to trust a woman to that extent, not even when he was a teenager. Even the mother he'd adored had lied to him as and when it had suited her to do so. His mother's first loyalty had always been to his father, no matter how badly the older man had treated either her or her son.

'Is that so?'

'Yes, that is so!' Leah proclaimed with spirit as she slid upright again, restless as a cat on hot bricks, to make the coffee he had forgotten about again. She might not be much of a cook, but she could manage coffee, couldn't she? She was shaken to see that her hands were trembling as she flipped through cupboards in search of china. Yes, there was a much bigger question looming over her blitzed brain. Would she or wouldn't she spend the night with the most sexually enthralling and gorgeous guy she had ever met?

In her restricted circle, when would such an opportunity ever present again? She didn't want to be an old and grey virgin, did she? And that *was* a distinct possibility, given the way she now felt about relationships, wasn't it? No man was ever going to get the chance to make a fool of her a second time!

'This proposal of yours…'

Brows pleating at that very word, Gio turned to look at her, surprised to see the now shuttered aspect of her vivid little face. 'Yes?'

Leah strengthened her backbone. She had been Oliver's doormat, silently swallowing his criticisms of her weight, her clothing choices, her accent and lack of culture. That would not be the blueprint for her future. From now on, intimacy of any kind would only happen on *her* terms and right now she could only contemplate the most superficial of bonds. 'If I agree,' she said tightly, 'it would be an agreement that it's a one-night stand and nothing more. I won't consider anything else.'

Gio laughed out loud in delight and astonishment combined, for no woman had ever offered him only one night without the potential for the connection to turn into something more. In that instant he decided that being Mr Nobody from Nowhere was sheer magic. Leah didn't want him for his money, his social position or his business influence because she was not aware of his true status, and while in other circumstances he might have considered it wrong not to admit who he was, when it came to one casual night he believed that nobody would be harmed by his decision to remain silent on that score.

'You think that what I said was funny?' Leah pressed tautly, taken aback by his amusement.

'Not in the sense that you suspect,' Gio told her confidently. 'Women can sometimes be a little clingy with me, so I was pleasantly surprised by your attitude and your directness.'

Leah could perfectly understand women getting clingy with a male as drop-dead beautiful as he was, but she was still encased in the protective armour that Oliver's deeply hurtful deception had inflicted on her. Her heart was now as frozen as any cartoon princess might wish for and, with it, any desire to *cling* to any man. To stay strong and safe, she reasoned, she needed to stand alone and control her own destiny, not allow either foolish romantic dreams or, worse, some self-serving male authority to influence her intelligence and her judgement again.

'Let me do that,' Gio interposed as she searched the entire kitchen, it seemed, for a teaspoon. 'Sit down—'

'Watch it. You're a bit too bossy for me,' Leah told him, a warning gleam in her caramel eyes.

Gio sent her a wolfish grin, thoroughly enjoying himself with a woman for the first time in a long time. All the size of her and trying to look tough, he acknowledged, impressed once again by that hint of an irrepressible spirit. He showed her the food he had put in a bowl for her dog and watched her attend to the little animal, before making the coffee and extending hers.

Leah was nonplussed by the level of his control, having dimly expected to be urged straight towards the nearest horizontal surface or whatever. She scolded herself for that naïve assumption. He wasn't an unpolished teenager keen to score at speed with the first available girl, he was rather more sophisticated.

Gio had never been so tempted to abandon all cool with a woman. Arousal was humming through every inch of his big powerful body. It was years since he had experienced anything like that level of desire in female company and he was determined to figure out what it was about Leah that revved him up to such an extent. A *ridiculous* extent, he told himself impatiently, when one conceded that he had never in his entire adult life been desperate for sex. So, what was it about her?

The vibrance of her expression? That amazing glossy mane of curls? The big dark eyes, whose expression she veiled when uncomfortable…like now? What the hell was she uncomfortable about? Telling him that the most he could expect from her was a one-night stand had been a pretty feisty move, not the behaviour of a shy or naïve woman, so why had that feisty assurance somehow struck a vaguely bogus note to his ears? *Dio*, was she one of those old-fashioned women, who still thought she had to play hard to get even as she surrendered to the same hunger that infused him?

Gio smiled and Leah was entrapped, instantly, irrevocably, watching the way that shift of his wide sculpted lips threw his exotic cheekbones into prominence and allowed those stunning eyes of his to narrow and glitter. Pale grey, she had thought at first, then she had tagged them as the palest possible blue with a near Mediterranean hint of turquoise when passion flared. A tiny shiver curled low in her pelvis and her whole body lit up like a firework display, forcing her to shift uneasily in her seat.

'I'm usually very good at restraint,' Gio told her truthfully. 'But right now, right here with you… I'm not feeling it, *cara.*'

His boldness made her feel outrageously shy, and she could feel her skin heating and tightening over her bones.

'You blush,' he said in apparent wonderment.

'Occasionally—'

'Will you blush if I ask you to come upstairs with me?'

'P-probably,' Leah muttered as he pushed away his untouched coffee and stood up to extend a hand to her. She tugged out her phone and sent a quick text to Sally, telling her that she wouldn't be home.

Her heart began to pound inside her as she too got up and reached for that hand, feeling rather like a drowning swimmer while fighting all those insecure feelings to the last ditch. So, this raw, powerful sense of connection was something new and different for her, but she would get used to it, being very adaptable as she had had to be throughout her life, she told herself firmly.

CHAPTER THREE

GIO PAUSED TO kiss Leah on the first landing because he, literally, couldn't keep his hands off her any longer. Passion flared like lightning, shooting through Leah like a jet-propelled rocket, both stunning and seducing, urging her arms round his neck without her realising how they had got there.

She was breathless and flushed as he walked her on up the next flight of steps, anticipation provoking a dull tugging ache at her feminine core. But for all that, she was disconcerted when he led her into what she had assumed was the master bedroom. 'Isn't this Mr Zanetti's room?' she exclaimed in surprise.

The faintest edge of colour scored Gio's cheekbones, because it was not a moment when he wished to be reminded of his whimsical impulse earlier to deny his true identity. 'He doesn't use this one,' he asserted, reaching for her again, determined to distract her from awkward questions while remaining unusually aware that he had just told an actual lie, which was not something he was in the habit of doing under any circumstances. *Harmless,* he reminded himself stubbornly as he collided with those wide dark eyes of hers with something weirdly similar to wonderment because *she* was making *him* act out of character. He didn't want to give her any excuse to walk away, but even less did he wish to see greed and ambition spark in her beautiful eyes.

But, usually, sex wasn't really that important to him, bearing in mind that it was always available to him no matter where he was because beautiful, willing potential partners were plentiful. As a rule, he didn't do one-night stands; he would stay with one woman for a couple of weeks and then move on before it got stale. It never lasted any longer than that, never got any deeper than that. He didn't offer commitment—indeed, since his short-lived marriage he had not surrendered or shared control in any element of his life. Sex was a trivial pursuit on the periphery of a driven life he devoted to technological research and business.

'Gianni...' she said, her soft voice purring along the syllables, and it was sufficient to spring him back out of that rare instant of introspection.

He kissed her again and the worry about whose room they were occupying melted away in a fresh tide of longing. Her T-shirt fell to the floor in the midst of a frantic bout of kissing, the zip of her shorts sliding down, the garment dropping to her ankles as he lifted her clear. She lay back on the bed where he placed her in a fevered daze, watching him dispense with sweater and jeans and toe off his boots to reveal an incredibly powerful physique, all lean, muscular strength and bronzed masculinity. He simply took her breath away. He was beautiful in a way she had never known a man could be, beautiful from his wide shoulders to his corrugated abdomen and long, strong legs.

As for the rest of him, she glossed her eyes over in haste because really there was rather more than she had dimly expected, but nature had made men and women to fit, so she wasn't going to stress about that aspect. He came back to her with a wolfish smile that blitzed her thoughts as much as his kisses because she was just enthralled, all her inexperience and insecurities overwhelmed by his breathtaking appeal.

'You are so beautiful,' Gio told her and, for

Leah, it seemed as though she had been waiting all her life for such words. She didn't believe it was true but on such an occasion he was allowed to exaggerate, she thought forgivingly.

Having released her hair from its topknot, Gio was watching that fabulous mane of black ringlets spill across the pillows, taking in the shining brilliance of her dark honey eyes, the reddened allure of her luscious mouth, and hunger took him by storm as he came down over her and ravished her lips again.

A little bit later, Leah discovered that her undergarments had magically disappeared, and the smoothness with which those items had been removed bothered her a little because it warned her that he was much more experienced than she was. And she didn't want to think about that for some reason she couldn't explain. She didn't like to think of the *other* women he had learned such skills from. And she knew that such a thought was ridiculous in a woman who had declared upfront that she was willing only to consider a one-night stand but there it was, denying her own feelings was beyond her: she was jealous as hell of any woman who had ever touched him.

'You're so quiet,' Gio purred, gazing down

at her with smouldering eyes semi-screened by lush black lashes.

'Do you know that you have lashes longer than the average girl's? No?' Leah went beet-red. 'That's *why* I should keep quiet—'

'I don't mind quirky,' Gio broke in with a surprised laugh of appreciation, big hands curving to the full firm curves of her breasts, thumbs gently skimming her prominent nipples. 'In fact quirky is refreshing.'

Rather belatedly, because everything had seemed to move so fast to her, Leah registered that she was naked for the very first time with a guy, and she could feel a wash of heat blossoming on her entire skin surface, but his touch on her sensitive peaks was sending an arrowing flame to the very heart of her, making her shift her hips under his weight. And then she could feel him against her, long and hard and urgent, and that ache between her thighs intensified.

Gio ran his lips down the side of her neck to where it met her shoulder and she gasped, because inexplicably that touch *there* seemed to light up her every nerve ending. She smelled like sunshine and fresh laundry, and he inhaled deeply, amazed by how evocative such natural scents could be. She panted as he lingered at her throat and tipped back as he glided lean fingers down over her quivering tummy, skated through the landing strip of curls below and circled the most sensitive spot on her whole body. Her spine arched, her teeth gritting on a powerful wave of response. He shimmied down the length of her and found the same place with his mouth and his fingers and his tongue.

'Oh…' Leah gasped, utterly awash in more sensation than she had ever known. It was as if a fierce pulse was beating through her while her heart thumped even faster, and she was so overpowered that she just closed her eyes tight and let the intoxicating wave of climbing pleasure take over.

Her reaction excited Gio as much as though he were with his very first woman and he was way too involved in that urgency to even consider what was so different. He raised himself to grab a condom from the nightstand by the bed and tore the foil open with his teeth, dimly acknowledging that he was struggling to stay in control while revelling in the excitement of that unique experience. Even the taste of her mouth drove him wild, he conceded, stealing another kiss with driven insistence, already knowing that no one-night stand was likely to sate him…but she'd change her mind about that, *of course* she would.

Leah felt him push past her tender entrance, even lifted herself a little as he canted up her hips and then he was driving into her, giving her what her entire being was keyed up to demand.

'You're so tight,' he proclaimed at almost the same moment as the burning stretch of his invasion became uncomfortable for her. A second later he withdrew to gain greater traction and drove back into her hard and fast. It hurt and she jerked just as he repeated the movement. The next time was less painful and, indeed, her breath caught in her throat in surprise when a renewed wave of hunger mixed with pleasure turned her pelvis into a cauldron of hot, melting liquidity.

His urgent rhythm ramped up her growing excitement. Her heart was thumping so hard it left her breathless. She wanted more, in fact her whole body was primed to a peak of burning need, so that every thrust of his body into hers felt agonisingly good and necessary. The surge of exhilaration engulfing her carried her to a dizzy high and then her body convulsed and broke into a million pieces and in the same instant she soared in an ecstasy of pleasure.

'Extraordinary,' Gio husked in her ear, dragging in a shuddering breath that shifted his broad chest against her, muscles rippling below his hair-roughened golden skin. He was bemused by the unexpected discovery that simple sex could be *that* good and a slashing smile at his own surprise lightened his lean, dark, serious features.

Leah looked up at him in a daze of satiation, struggling to hide a surprise even stronger than his because until that moment she truly hadn't thought she had missed out on much by not experimenting more. He eased back from her to spring out of the bed and then registered that for the first time ever his precautions had failed him.

'Are you using contraception?' he asked tautly.

Leah blinked in consternation. She had taken the pill the whole time she was with Oliver on the assumption that eventually their relationship would become more physical, only it hadn't done and in frustration at that lowering truth she had dumped her pills after he ditched her. 'Er…no,' she muttered awkwardly.

'Unluckily for us, the condom broke,' Gio told her as he slid out of the bed, only then seeing the smear of blood on his thigh. He froze and lifted pale glittering eyes to her mortified face. 'Would it be crazy of me to ask if you were a virgin?'

As the ramifications of what he had told her set in, Leah cringed in sharp dismay. Nobody knew more about unplanned pregnancies and their unwelcome consequences than Leah, who had grown up virtually without a father. 'We don't have to talk about that,' she murmured flatly. 'And we may have had an accident, but I doubt that anything will come of it…my system's irregular.'

'Right,' Gio breathed between gritted teeth, already blaming himself for not having discussed contraception beforehand with her. Checking that his partner was additionally protected was an extra precaution he had practised for years after his divorce. Unhappily he had stopped being that careful because no such accident had ever occurred to him before. But what were the odds of conception? he asked himself with sudden impatience. One mishap, one chance, pretty good odds in his favour, he decided, repressing any further concern.

Without further ado, Gio disappeared into the bathroom and Leah flopped back weakly against the pillows, trying not to recall her mother, who had once joked that she was fertile enough to fall pregnant just by looking at the wrong man. Oh, why, oh, why had she stopped taking the pill? But she knew *why.* At the time she hadn't envisaged ever being with a man and certainly not on a casual basis. Regret and insecurity threatened and, in the midst of that attack, Leah leapt out of bed and began to scrabble for her clothes at speed.

'What are you doing?' Gio asked from the doorway.

'I thought I'd take a shower downstairs and then go home—'

Gio reached for the hands she had filled with her clothes and she fumbled to continue holding them, but they fell to the polished floor. 'I don't want you to leave... I want you to stay.'

Disconcerted, Leah clashed with the silvered glitter of eyes bright as diamonds in his lean, darkly handsome face. Her heart performed a somersault and her tummy shimmied with butterflies. His tousled dark head lowered to hers and her hands went up into his hair to tug him down to her. The need to touch him again was frighteningly instinctive and it had nothing at all to do with the defensive 'let's escape' urge that had been controlling her only seconds earlier. His mouth claimed and captured hers and her head swam and her knees wobbled as an intoxicating rush of hunger awakened every nerve ending afresh…

Dawn was the merest hint beyond the blinds when Leah woke up. Her lashes fluttered with confusion until she remembered and then she almost groaned out loud at the embarrassing prospect of having to rise and finish cleaning the house while the male beside her was still in residence. She eased out of bed with all the nimble quietness of a cat burglar, gathered up the clothes she had dropped and crept downstairs. Spike was waiting at the foot of the stairs for her.

Dressed after a lick and promise of a brief wash in the cloakroom, she registered the time and decided to try and finish the outstanding work before departing. Once she had one of the solid mahogany doors closed, the noise she made would not carry far, she reasoned, heading quickly into the nearest room with her implements. No, she wasn't going to have regrets, she told herself. What was done was done. She wasn't about to slut-shame herself for doing something that most women had done long before her. She had made a decision and she stood by it.

Having dusted at speed, she winced as she had to stretch to vacuum a corner. She ached all over; she ached as though she had run a marathon overnight. Her face burned. He had proved to be sexually demanding but he had made the whole experience a positive one. He had been respectful and considerate, and she was grateful for that. That aside, however, the passion, the wild intensity of their encounter had shocked her.

Gio sat up in the empty bed and glanced at his watch with a frown. He had slept in and that was most unlike him. He studied the space where Leah had been and his frown grew even darker. Where was she? He rarely spent the whole night with a woman and, since he had chosen to do so with her, her absence irked him. A faint noise from the ground floor, however, followed by a low wuffly little bark, released his tension and made him smile. Vaulting out of bed, he went for a shower. He would tell Leah the truth, he conceded as the water pounded him. Being Mr Nobody from Nowhere had been entertaining, but it was a lie and he could not continue lying to her, at least not if he intended to spend more time with her. An empty weekend loomed ahead of him and he could see no reason why he should not spend it with Leah. True, it had not seemed empty before he had met her, he conceded; indeed he *had* been looking forward to his own company.

Leah reeled in the vacuum cord with a sigh of relief. Her back was sore, her mouth dry, her tummy running on empty because she had not dared to stop to eat or drink. She was exhausted after working at top speed following a night during which she had only enjoyed snatches of sleep. The reward, however, was that she had pretty much completed the basic clean Pam had requested and now she could go home.

The door opened just as she lifted the vacuum cleaner and she froze, before noisily setting it down again, her oval face flushing from the intensity of Gio's scrutiny. In casual cargo pants and an open-necked black shirt, he somehow contrived to look ridiculously sophisticated…and gorgeous. His lean bronzed features were classic from his high cheekbones, narrow masculine nose and sculpted mouth. He was undeniably sheer masculine perfection. And just that one look and she felt giddy.

'I've fed Spike and made coffee,' he informed her with a faint smile that turned his handsome mouth up at the corners and exuded an incredible amount of barefaced charm.

'Thanks for Spike…but I'd already fed him. He's a trickster. He always acts like he's starving,' she gabbled, her hand tightening on the cleaning box she still held. 'Unfortunately, I was just about to go home—'

'Give me ten minutes,' Gio bargained. 'There's something I have to tell you.'

What on earth could he have to tell her? Oh, my goodness, was he about to confess that he had a girlfriend? Even worse, a wife? Her empty tummy hollowed out sickly. Was it weak of her to feel like telling him that she really didn't want to know now that it was too late to change anything? Conscious of him on her heels, she stowed the cleaning box in the pantry and went back to retrieve the vacuum. She put away the vacuum, knowing that she just wanted to run but that that would be gauche, and she wasn't still that immature, was she? Perspiration had broken out on her short upper lip as she returned to the kitchen, her car keys jangling in her pocket.

'What's the problem?' Leah prompted stiffly.

Gio studied her, entranced by her beautiful eyes, the tumble of black curls surrounding her eloquent little face and the very bossy, purposeful bustle of her movements when she was working. Nothing was studied, nothing faked for glossy presentation or sex appeal. Everything about Leah was so *real*, from the shadows below her eyes to her curvy, wondrous shape. There was nothing gym-honed about the softness of her against him either. A surge of intense lust hit him, disconcerting him with the speed of that renewal.

'I don't see why it should be a problem,' Gio told her truthfully, for he had never heard a woman lament the discovery that her lover was a billionaire, 'but, unfortunately, I wasn't entirely frank with you when we first met last night.'

'Frank?' Leah queried the word uncertainly.

'I didn't want things to be awkward, so I said that I worked for Gio Zanetti when, in fact, I *am* Giovanni Zanetti,' Gio spelled out.

Leah's tummy was churning, her skin turning clammy with shock. 'You said your name was Gianni…'

'That was true. Both Gio and Gianni are diminutives of Giovanni, although the latter name was only ever used by family,' he conceded.

Leah had turned pale as death because she really couldn't credit that this was happening to her again: a man lying to her about who and what he was. What was it about her? Did she have stupid, trusting fool stamped on her forehead?

'You're saying that you're the… Gazillionaire?' she almost whispered.

Gio was struggling to work out why Leah was looking at him in horror. It wasn't embarrassment or annoyance. It was more like the response he might have expected had he announced that he was a serial killer. 'Yes, but telling you that yesterday when I surprised you in the pool would have been more upsetting for you—'

'No,' Leah framed. 'It would have been the truth.'

'The truth isn't always welcome,' Gio countered without apology. 'I would have had to read the Riot Act about you being in the pool.'

Leah parted bloodless lips. 'Better that than lying to me. You let me think you were someone else and then you slept with me. That is unforgivable.'

'I hope that you don't mean that,' Gio commented smoothly. 'Once I had claimed to be an employee I was stuck with that story.'

'Otherwise, I might not have slept with you,' Leah suggested.

Pale eyes as bright as diamonds below a lush curtain of black lashes inspected her. 'I don't think that would have been an issue.'

'I don't like liars,' Leah almost whispered, stepping past him to scoop up Spike from his position in the hallway. 'I would never have spent the night with you if I had known you had lied to me.'

Gio frowned. 'You're making far too much of this. I saved us from an awkward moment with a harmless lie. At that stage I had no idea that we were going to end up in bed together and now I've come clean—'

Leah shot him a furious glance from her dark eyes. 'It wasn't harmless. You're not the man I thought you were. There's a huge chasm between who you are and who you pretended to be. I wouldn't have got into bed with the Gazillionaire—'

'I'm apologising!' Gio broke in, his dark drawl raw-edged. 'I am truly sorry that I misled you and I promise that I will not tell the smallest untruth from this minute forward.'

Spike tucked under her arm, her bag over her shoulder, Leah tugged open the back door. 'It doesn't matter anyway. It was a one-night thing—'

'I don't *want* it to be.'

Leah spun back to him, volatile sparks in her angry gaze. 'You accepted it last night… so you *lied* about that as well?'

'Most women aren't offended when a man wants to spend more time in their company—'

'I'm not *most* women!' Leah hissed and turned on her heel again to march out into the courtyard.

'You're telling me,' Gio muttered in gritty agreement under his breath.

Pausing at the side of the shabby old hatchback parked nearby, Leah stared back at him. 'I don't want to see you or hear from you ever again!' she declared as she stowed her bag and carefully installed the dog in the carrier box in the back seat.

As she drove off, grinding through the gears and executing a noisy handbrake turn, Gio swallowed back an astonished laugh. She was a hellish rough driver and she had an even more hellish temper. How many years was it since a woman had censured him? Refused him? Turned her nose up at an apology? Acted difficult? He couldn't remember. In fact, he couldn't remember that *ever* happening to him, even during his divorce. Gabriella had been sweet as sugar throughout the negotiations while she'd robbed him blind after only a few short months of matrimony. He had been hung out to dry by the gold-digger he had married without ever putting a foot wrong...

CHAPTER FOUR

THE NERVE OF HIM! Leah thought furiously as she drove away from Shore House. Gio/Gianni/Giovanni Zanetti had run rings around her. She had not suspected a thing. And there he had been, cool as ice and full of lies and deception just like Oliver! Never again would she even contemplate a guy who told her anything but the truth because she had learned the hard way that lies cut her deep. Left her with scars she couldn't shake, rubbished her pride and filled her with insecurity and self-doubt.

Sally's eyes were bright with curiosity as Leah walked in the back door.

'Least said, soonest mended,' Leah quipped ruefully.

'A mistake?' her foster mother prompted.

'Partially,' Leah agreed after a reflective pause. 'But not important in the scheme of things.'

Sally winced and then smiled. 'Well, I'm not about to pry.'

Relief swept Leah. She had called in with Pam on her way home and had reported back on the state of Shore House without mentioning Gio's early arrival there. Then she had collected Pam's prescription and promised to return the next day to cut the lawn. Changing into her oldest clothes, she went out to the rackety collection of old buildings that housed the rescue animals and helped one of Sally's keen volunteers to clean out inmates that ranged from goats and rabbits to cats and dogs.

When she came back indoors for lunch, Sally sent her a veiled appraisal and murmured, 'Pam phoned. Mr Zanetti will be calling here this afternoon.'

Leah flushed to the roots of her hair. 'Yes. It was him and he's…persistent—'

'Oh, dear,' Sally said without turning a hair. 'Do you want me to deal with him?'

'No, thanks. I can handle him,' Leah breathed, more embarrassed than ever.

'You should get changed,' her former foster mother remarked, eying Leah's ancient jeans and tatty T-shirt with a frown.

'No. I'll do fine as I am,' Leah declared, lifting her chin.

Gio Zanetti drew up in a Bugatti Centodieci, a long, ridiculously sleek white sports car that looked as though it would be far more at home on a racetrack than a narrow country lane. It was Sally, who had an interest in cars, who excitedly told her what it was and what it was likely worth.

'What a show-off he is!' Leah commented, determined not to be impressed.

She walked stiff-backed to the front door and opened it, watching as Gio swung gracefully out of his phenomenally expensive vehicle. Sunlight gleamed over his black hair and bronzed skin, accentuating his classic bone structure and the piercing brilliance of light eyes set below level ebony brows. His physical impact was intense, she acknowledged, her tummy clenching with nerves and her heart hammering. She breathed in slow and deep. 'Mr Zanetti…' she said.

'Really?' Gio hitched a satirical brow. 'Is that how we're playing it?'

'I don't know what you're doing here,' Leah admitted tightly.

Gio strolled towards her. 'Evidently, my interest in you is less fleeting than yours in me… or so you would have me believe—'

'So, vanity brought you here,' Leah contended waspishly.

'No, the way you look at me even now brought me here and keeps me here,' Gio countered with a slashing confident smile. '*Dio mio*…what is the problem?'

In receipt of that smile her mouth ran dry and something in her pelvis heated, tightened and clenched in the most intimate way. 'I didn't say there was one, only that one night was as much as I could contemplate—'

'*Please* change your mind,' Gio urged, staring down at her with those extraordinary eyes that made her head swim. He lifted a hand to trace the outline of her mouth with a caressing finger and instant heat flooded her as she stood there, her physical response a screaming denial of everything she had told him.

'I can't,' she whispered unevenly.

And he bent his head and the pulse at the heart of her kicked up, flaring in anticipation. His mouth came down on her slowly, touching, brushing, tasting, and her hand came up to rest on his chest, feeling the fast beat of his heart. Hunger flooded her in an intoxicating wave as his tongue dallied with hers and she felt him, hard and ready against her, his long, lean, strong body as taut as her own. She wanted, *needed*…

Gio stepped back. 'Leah?' he breathed roughly.

'You lied and I couldn't forgive that,' Leah admitted tightly.

'You're a vengeful little soul, aren't you?' Gio murmured with grim amusement as he extended something to her.

'What's this?' Leah muttered, staring down at the black and gold business card he had handed her, her body still quivering from that kiss that had liquefied her bones and filled her with an almost unbearable craving.

'My phone number. In case you change your mind… *Buongiorno*, Spike, better luck next time,' Gio said in an aside as the little dog tried and failed to get his mouth into the back of his denim-clad calf, and then turned back to her to add, 'Or should there be consequences for the little mishap we had.'

Leah was struggling to understand how he could be so hot and sexy and yet make her want to slap him at the same time, but at that reminder she lost colour and dug the card into her pocket. 'Unlikely,' she replied flatly.

'That's some powerful chemistry,' Sally commented, coming up behind her as Gio drove off. 'Takes some backbone to say no to that.'

'No...it only takes common sense,' Leah contradicted tautly.

In the aftermath of the sickness, Leah freshened up, grimacing at her watering eyes and her pallor in the mirror. She looked awful, felt worse, if that were possible. And she was only twenty weeks pregnant. Her fond belief that what had happened to her mother wouldn't happen to her had been foolish. She had conceived and now she had to deal with her plight. For the past month after the doctor had confirmed her suspicions and outlined her options, Leah had been lost inside her own head, making and discarding unrealistic plans.

From an early stage she had known that she would keep her baby and raise it. She had lost her entire family growing up but now she felt as though she was receiving a second chance at having a family and nobody was going to take that opportunity away from her. True, the way she was having her first child, alone and without support, was far from being ideal. But, sometimes, life threw up the unexpected and it had to be handled. She was excited about her baby and didn't feel that she could freely express that truth because becoming a young single mother put her into a category that some liked to mock and deride.

Sally, predictably, wanted her to stay with her to have the baby but Leah was determined that the older woman should not pay for *her* carelessness. And a young child in the household would definitely be an added burden. Rediscovering her independence, Leah reflected, was a necessity.

For that reason she was moving back to London to take up a live-in job as a companion/carer for an elderly woman. Sally had argued vehemently about that decision, but Leah knew that it was time to stand on her own feet again. She had no idea as yet what she would do to support herself after her baby was born but thought that, with her business degree, she might be able to find paid employment that allowed her to work remotely. If she was able to support herself, she would be willing to move back in with Sally then.

It was also time that she informed Gio Zanetti that in a few months' time he would be a father. She had no idea how he would feel about that, but she acknowledged his right to know. Keep it impersonal, she urged herself, that being the attitude she had sworn to take. He was unlikely to be pleased at her news but then she wasn't that pleased either that the father of her child was a liar.

Recalling that truth, she lifted her chin and reached for her phone because she had been putting off contacting Gio for long enough.

'It's Leah,' she announced when he answered. 'Leah Ramsay. We met at Shore House.'

'I haven't forgotten,' he intoned, his dark deep drawl shimmying down her spine and up again, sending a ridiculous little shiver of awareness through her.

'I need to see you to discuss something—'

'*Something?*' a faint chilling note laced his intonation.

'I won't take up much of your time. Ten minutes at most,' Leah asserted tightly. 'I'll be in London in two weeks.'

'I'll text you an address and a time,' Gio responded flatly and rang off.

Well, that was short and sweet, Leah conceded ruefully. Had he guessed? She supposed it was better all-round if he had, at least, an inkling. Thirty minutes later, her phone buzzed with the address of an apartment building and a time that suited her.

It was a very fancy apartment block with that sleek elegant air that just screamed expense.

Fresh from moving into her damp bedsit in a basement, Leah was less well groomed than she had planned to be. Since her return to London she had been very busy completing a long list of tasks for her new employer. Mrs Evans was a kind woman, independent and pleasant, but her reluctance to bother her daughter with constant requests had ensured that many of her needs went unmet until Leah's arrival.

Leah wore jeans, a jazzy long-sleeved top and ankle boots, a practical outfit she had donned for a shopping trip, and she carried a bag crammed with the craft supplies she had collected for her elderly charge. Gio occupied the penthouse suite and an older man dressed like an old-fashioned manservant answered the door and ushered her through an opulent foyer into a large lounge area, decorated in tranquil greys with flashes of turquoise. The luxury was quiet and understated but she was very much aware of feeling that she did not belong in such a rarefied milieu. There Gio awaited her, spinning round from a tall window overlooking a leafy roof garden to study her with narrowed mercury-bright eyes.

Her heart began to hammer inside her chest, her mouth drying, her tummy tightening. It had only been a few months, but she had still contrived to forget the intensity of his physical impact and the spectacular good looks that literally stopped her in her tracks. Every honed and chiselled inch of him commanded her attention. There was nothing laid-back about either his appearance or his stance, not the smallest hint of informality or relaxation. He was sheathed in a beautifully cut charcoal suit that fitted him to perfection, outlining broad shoulders, lean hips and long, strong legs. A dark blue shirt was set off by a grey tie. Tension was etched into the hard cast of his lean, darkly handsome features, his bronzed skin taut over his slashing cheekbones and strong sculpted jaw. He had guessed, she registered, he had guessed what she was coming to tell him. But even that knowledge could not prevent the demeaning tightening at the heart of her or the prickling of her nipples, the soaring shameless surge of sexual awareness that she could not suppress.

Gio scrutinised her with innate concentration. She was paler than he remembered, smaller too, but the tumbled black curls, the beautiful eyes and clear creamy skin were unchanged, and hunger sparked in him at unnerving speed, intimate recollections teasing at the edges of his usually disciplined mind.

He hadn't forgotten her, no, he certainly hadn't forgotten her in spite of every effort to do so.

He shifted position, irritated by the warning throb at his groin, inwardly talking himself down from that sexual edge while questioning what it was about her that so easily revved his engine. She had walked away from him and he wasn't used to rejection, at least not since he was a child. Back then he had met with rejection at every corner. Rejection from neighbours, classmates, teachers, from all those people who could see him only as the loser son of a vicious drug dealer, guaranteed to follow in his papa's footsteps. He had learned early to fight rejection and simply accepting it was still a challenge for him. But he had not chased Leah, he had respected her decision, which made the current situation all the more infuriating. Gio preferred to be in charge when trouble kicked off…and if she was about to tell him what he assumed, it *was* trouble.

'Obviously you're here to tell me that you're pregnant,' Gio murmured coolly, his silvery gaze tough and penetrating as steel. 'But that's not a discussion I'm willing to have with you yet—'

Taken aback by that blunt opening speech,

Leah paled. 'It's...*not*?' she heard herself say in confusion.

'No, it would be pointless for us to discuss anything without proof—'

'Proof that I'm pregnant?' Leah queried. 'You know, it would have been nice if you had at least greeted me, asked me how I am and invited me to take a seat—'

'I don't do nice in these circumstances, but you are, of course, welcome to sit down,' Gio breathed tautly. 'My apologies, if my business-like approach has offended you.'

'It hasn't,' Leah hastened to assure him, although she could feel the heat of mortification rising over her skin in betrayal of that brave claim and she felt too uncomfortable to take a seat.

'To answer your question,' Gio continued smoothly, 'no, I didn't mean proof that you're pregnant, I meant proof that any child you may be carrying is *my* child—something which can easily be established by a simple DNA test. We each give a blood sample at a laboratory and paternity can be established right now.'

Her eyes widened with bewilderment. 'Why would paternity have to be established?'

'Let's not be naïve,' Gio urged very drily. 'You've waited a long time to tell me that you're pregnant. You could be pregnant by some other man you met *after* you were with me.'

All the heat in Leah's skin retreated, leaving her very pale. She blinked rapidly, biting back an angry response. Not since she had broken up with Oliver had she felt so insulted or humiliated. Gio seemed to be insinuating that her very first sexual experience had set her on some immediate path of loose living in which she moved on very quickly from him to sample other men. 'I haven't been with anyone else. I've only been with you—'

'Surely you understand that I can't just take your word for that?' Gio shot back at her arrogantly.

'No. I'm afraid I don't accept that,' Leah countered stiffly. 'Not at this stage anyway. After all, I require nothing from you while I'm pregnant. I only contacted you now and came to tell you that I was pregnant because I felt that you had the right to know. Now that I've done that, I'll leave again.'

Gio stared at her in growing frustration. He was being realistic, totally realistic in his request that she take a DNA test to prove that her pregnancy was *his* responsibility. 'Are you saying that you refuse to take that test?'

'Right at this moment, I think it is humiliating for you to expect me to take a test when the only reason I'm here is to tell you that I'm pregnant,' Leah countered tightly. 'It's unnecessary and I won't agree to it. When the baby is born I will agree to a DNA test, not before. For the present you can keep your nasty suspicions that I could be trying to con you in some way to yourself.'

'I didn't make such an accusation,' Gio parried curtly, a hint of colour highlighting his exotic cheekbones. 'Women have been known to make an honest mistake in that line and I think it is wiser to establish the truth from the outset.'

Leah shrugged a slight shoulder, not prepared to concede that she was at fault because she could tell from his reaction that in some way she had drawn blood with her words, just as he had done with his. She supposed that made them even and each of them knew where the other stood, even if it was on opposing sides. Even if it had taken her a long time, she had done her duty in telling him about their baby. It was up to him if he chose not to believe her. 'We can agree to differ,' she murmured flatly and began to turn on her heel.

'Are you still living with your foster mother?'

Leah glanced back at him. 'No. I'm back in London.'

'I'd like to have your address.'

Grudgingly, she gave it and he put it into his phone.

Leah returned to her bedsit with the lowering sense that she had the weight of the world on her shoulders. She didn't know what she had expected from Gio but it had not occurred to her that he would question that any child she had conceived was his. She had been naïve, she told herself ruefully. He was a very wealthy man, probably used to people trying to take advantage of him. But no matter how much she tried to make excuses for him, she could only think of how alone she felt in her current predicament and how small and somehow soiled his attitude had made her feel. For that reason it was wonderful that evening to receive a phone call from Sally, asking if it was all right to pass on her contact details to a solicitor, who was keen to get in touch with Leah, concerning 'a confidential family matter'.

Leah's heart leapt with hope at that information, and she urged her foster mother to give her address and phone number to the solicitor. Was it possible that after all this time her twin brother or her kid sister could be trying to find her?

* * *

A busy two weeks passed as Leah settled into her job. She missed Spike terribly, but she had not been able to bring him with her. Towards the end of the second week she received a call from the solicitor offering her an appointment at an office in central London. Infused with curiosity, Leah attended, only to immediately recognise by the older woman's grave demeanour that she might be about to receive bad news. And so it proved.

Leah learned that her father had passed away several years earlier. As she had barely a blurred memory of the man, the discovery suffused her with only bemused sadness, more regret for what might have been than true grief. The announcement that her half-brother, Ari Stefanos, wished to meet her had a much more powerful effect on her. She was stunned by that idea, having always assumed that her father's legitimate son would want nothing to do with his children by another woman.

She was even more pleased to learn that Ari had been trying to trace her siblings as well and indeed that he had already had some success in that field. Finding out that her twin brother, Lucas, had died from a drug overdose was a crushing blow and a wrenching disappointment for her, however. She had last seen Lucas when she was a student, by which time his substance abuse had made him almost unrecognisable. He had stolen their mother's jewellery from her, presumably to sell the items and buy drugs. Leah had been devastated to lose those keepsakes, particularly as nothing in that small collection had been valuable. Even then she had suspected that her twin's addiction would eventually kill him and had felt hammered with guilt that she could not get through to him and change his outlook and habits.

By the time she had expressed keen interest in meeting her half-brother, Ari, Leah was in a daze and increasingly upset by the discovery that she had lost her twin for ever. The little boy she remembered playing with so innocently was no more and it broke her heart that her twin had been unable to cope with the world he found himself in to the extent that he had tried to block it out with his addiction.

When the solicitor went on to inform her that she had been left a large sum of money by her late father, she was very much taken aback. Discovering that the man she had barely known and whose name she had no longer recalled because it was not on her birth certificate had left her several million pounds bereft her of breath and she struggled to accept the concept of her sudden wealth, because she had lived her entire life stressing about money. She signed the document extended to her in a state of astonishment. Only as she travelled back home did she process the idea of having inherited sufficient money to have choices that she had never had before.

And thanks to that inheritance, her child would never know the insecurity that had been Leah's lot from an early age. Sudden intense relief assailed her, piercing and lightening the veil of grief that had consumed her. Perhaps she would buy a house somewhere near Sally or some sort of small business that would provide her with an income. She felt wonderfully liberated by the truth that she would not need Gio Zanetti's financial help to survive.

When the doorbell rang early that evening, she was surprised because her employer already had a friend visiting with her. It was a shock to open the door to Gio. Leah froze in the doorway, her lips parting in surprise, her heart hammering as if she were engaged in a race and rushing to the finishing line.

'What are you doing here?' she asked helplessly, intimidated by the sheer size of him that close. In the dusk light, his stunning eyes were pure silver, enhanced by lush black lashes as effective as eyeliner. He was gorgeous, particularly with a dark shadow of stubble outlining his stubborn mouth and jaw, arrestingly masculine, shockingly sexy. As always, that lean bronzed face momentarily froze her to the spot. A lot of good that sexiness had done her, Leah scolded herself impatiently.

'I wanted to check that you were OK,' Gio advanced with precision, connecting with eyes as intriguing as tiger's eye gemstones, brown streaked with warm gold and honey, striking in their colour and intensity. The passion she couldn't hide drew him like a burning flame on a cold day. He was learning that it didn't matter that she wore no make-up, that her hair was tousled and her clothing unflattering. None of those facts mattered when it came to the fierce sexual blaze she lit inside him.

'Why wouldn't I be?' she asked defensively.

'May I come in?'

Leah wanted to say no but reckoned that would be pointlessly provocative and there was no advantage to being on bad terms with the father of her child. 'I suppose so...'

While wishing for a little more enthusiasm on her part, Gio lifted his proud dark head high and moved past her into the confined hallway. He had obeyed a random prompting to visit her unannounced and was unusually uncertain of his motives. 'I was concerned. I need to know you're all right and that you have everything you need. This is not a good area for you to be living in—'

'I don't go out much at night, so that's not a concern. You'd better come downstairs,' she sighed, leading the way down the twisting steep stairs into the basement area, which smelt of damp and disuse.

She opened the door reluctantly into her scrupulously tidy bedroom. Gio skimmed his gaze over the drab little room, taking in the signs of damp in one corner and grimacing. 'You shouldn't be living like this while you're pregnant. It's not healthy.'

'I'm fine. I shan't be staying much longer anyway. In fact, I'm about to hand in my notice.'

Gio frowned. 'Why? You've only been here a week or so, haven't you?'

'My circumstances are changing,' Leah stated grudgingly. 'It was unexpected.'

'How?' Gio asked bluntly.

'I don't think you're entitled to ask me personal questions,' Leah told him thinly.

'If you are carrying my baby, I am naturally going to feel responsible for your welfare,' Gio imparted curtly.

'But it positively shines out of you that you don't *want* this to be your baby or to feel responsible!' Leah snapped back at him, her voice rising slightly in volume.

'Does any single man really want to become a father after one fleeting encounter with a woman who wants nothing more to do with him?' Gio enquired very drily.

Colour stung her cheeks. 'It wasn't that I wanted nothing more to do with you—'

'It was,' Gio incised. 'Don't try to wrap it up. Best to be honest in our current circumstances.'

'Look, it wasn't like that,' Leah protested, feeling unexpectedly guilty when he described their brief connection in such terms. 'It was the fact that you concealed your identity and lied. I had had a recent bad experience with someone who had lied to me throughout our relationship and what you did reminded me of that and that unnerved me.'

'I am very sorry that I pretended to be an

ordinary working guy. I lied on impulse without thinking it through. I didn't think I'd ever see you again at that point,' Gio imparted with decided sincerity.

Leah nodded as though she understood and accepted his explanation when in truth she was neither so understanding nor so forgiving after Oliver's deception. Oliver had destroyed her faith in her own judgement. Even before Oliver, her trust in the male sex had been seriously damaged by her father's irresponsibility as a parent and her brother's many broken promises and lies. She had once been so infatuated with Oliver and his status as a high-flying lawyer that she had swallowed his every word as though it were gospel. And the very memory of that weakness, that lack of judgement, still shamed Leah in her own eyes.

'I wasn't ready for another relationship anyway,' Leah summarised, keen to drop the subject since she did not want to argue with him and create bad feeling for no good reason.

'I've been there,' Gio breathed, with sudden darkness shadowing his handsome features. 'What happened to you?'

'I once fell for someone who was lying to me from the day that we met,' she muttered uncomfortably, not wishing to explain how blind she had been to Oliver's unscrupulous character and behaviour.

It was not as though she were stupid and yet how else could she interpret her failure to spot Oliver as the cheat, liar and master manipulator that he had been? Oliver's moral compass had been non-existent.

The suspicion that he was virtually paying for some other man's mistreatment of her could only infuriate Gio and he gritted his teeth on the temptation to tell her so. A phone rang out a noisy rocky tune and she dug it out of her pocket to answer it.

'Oh…' she said slowly in a tone of great surprise and then suddenly she smiled, her whole face lighting up. 'Like…*right now*?'

Mystified but genuinely excited to hear the voice of her newly discovered half-brother greeting her, Leah moved back towards her bedroom door, amused as Ari apologised profusely for his eagerness to meet her for the first time. He even told her how his wife had tried to restrain him by telling him not to crowd her on the same day that she had already had bad news delivered. A tiny giggle bubbled from Leah's lips.

'I wasn't expecting to hear from you so soon and *this* is good news,' she murmured softly, thinking that he was family and family was something she had craved for a long time. 'Problem is I don't really have anywhere to entertain you here...oh, yes, I can do that... If you feed me as well, I'm yours for ever! Ten minutes? I'll be waiting!'

Switching off her phone, she dug it back into her pocket and turned to look at Gio with colour brightening her formerly pale cheeks. 'I'm afraid I've got an unexpected invitation out that I would like to accept—'

'I was only dropping in,' Gio conceded with a rather jerky shrug of dismissal when all he wanted to know was who had put the blush into her cheeks and lit up her big dark eyes like stars. By her enthusiasm, he assumed the caller was male and he didn't like the direction his thoughts were travelling in one little bit.

He followed her back up the stairs, a knot of trapped rage starting to burn in his gut. He had been right to demand the DNA test and wise to call on her without warning. If he hadn't done so, he wouldn't have realised that she had another man in her life.

'I'll keep in touch,' he breathed tautly at the front door.

'If you like but it's not necessary right now,' Leah told him abstractedly.

Gio strode back to his car in a very bad mood, turbulent emotions washing through him in waves. As the front door shut he stayed static before stretching back in his seat to wait. Barely ten minutes later, a limousine double-parked, and a tall dark male leapt out and strode to the door. A light came on illuminating his features and incredulous recognition gripped Gio. Ari Stefanos! What the hell was Leah doing with a very married Greek billionaire? Could he be the man Leah had fallen for who had lied to her from the day they had met?

Gio watched the front door open, Leah's face unexpectedly serious as taut first words were exchanged and then she started crying and literally hurled herself into Stefanos' waiting arms. Gio wanted to get out and kill both of them stone dead where they stood. The sick sense of betrayal almost ate him alive. He hadn't felt like that since his marriage and bitterness almost consumed him. Why hadn't Leah been honest with him? Was the child she carried the Greek's? And if so, when had she first got together with him? The facts didn't match his suspicions, he grasped dimly.

CHAPTER FIVE

ARI PUT UP with Leah sobbing into his chest remarkably well and once she had recovered from her emotional reaction to his telling her that she reminded him very much of his little sister, who had died when he was a child, she told her employer that she would be back by midnight, before fetching her coat and bag and climbing into her brother's limo with him to be taken back to his London home, where she would meet his wife, Cleo…and some other surprise he had yet to specify for her benefit.

'So, satisfy my curiosity if you can,' Ari urged. 'How on earth did my father and your mother meet? I can't discover any evidence that she ever worked for him—'

'Oh, no, she didn't work for him. They both joined a bereavement group and that's how they met. He had lost your sister and Mum had lost her only sibling to cancer,' Leah explained. 'She told me the whole story shortly before she died. Mum believed that your father was separated from your mother when their affair began but I don't think he was entirely honest with her. Mum conceived my brother and I very early on and their relationship continued. I don't think it was the romance of the century. I think it was more lonely, unhappy people getting together when life was tough. I have vague memories of your father but he's not on my birth certificate and he stopped visiting when I was still very young. To be honest I couldn't even recall his name until the solicitor said it because it had been so long since I had heard it—'

'I don't know what possessed my father. He let you all down badly as a parent and yet—'

'I think your parents' marriage was in a bad way when he first met my mother but then the situation changed—'

'My mother had a nervous breakdown—'

'Did she? Well, anyway, Mum said he pretty much vanished for months and when he reappeared she broke things off with him for good and moved away to make a fresh start. By then she knew there was no future in the relationship, and she didn't want ties with him,' Leah told him wryly. 'Unfortunately, she only then discovered that she was expecting my little sister, Eloise, and Eloise was a newborn when Mum died.'

'Eloise was adopted. I've lodged a letter asking for contact with the agency involved, but she has to ask for contact first. She's over eighteen now, so we'll have to wait and see what happens.' Ari sighed. 'I don't have a lot of patience, unfortunately.'

'Neither do I,' Leah quipped. 'Maybe it's a family trait.'

She was chattering freely by the time they arrived at her brother's imposing town house, and meeting her sister-in-law, Cleo, a warm, welcoming and noticeably pregnant young woman with guinea gold curls, only increased Leah's level of comfort. She was stunned when Ari explained that her late brother and his girlfriend, who had died with him, had had a child together and that he and Cleo had adopted little Lucy. A stinging rush of tears glossed Leah's eyes when Cleo brought a tiny girl into the room to join them for dinner. She was so cute and the knowledge that this child was her niece and her brother's living legacy almost overwhelmed her. She was deeply touched that Ari had had a big enough heart to bring Lucy into his family, fully accepting the bond of blood that some men would have disdained as beneath their notice.

The warmth she sensed in her brother and his wife quickly won her trust, and, when Ari confessed that he had had to have her investigated thoroughly to find her and that he already knew that she was pregnant, she respected his honesty and was willing to give a frank account of what had happened with Gio. Ari invited her out to stay in his home in Greece while Cleo urged her to make an appointment to see the same obstetrician she used.

'I'm giving notice that I'm leaving but I can't leave Mrs Evans in the lurch,' Leah declared apologetically.

Luckily for her, Ari had a solution for every problem. He told her that he would bring in a qualified carer to take her place and free her up from her job sooner. He was very set on taking her and his family out to his Greek island, Spinos, where they could relax and take the time to get to know each other. Leah, in turn, was curious to see the island that her father had once called home and learn more about her paternal background.

When she arrived home at midnight, her thoughts were in a spin and she climbed into bed and slept like a log. Her phone rang while she was bringing Mrs Evans her breakfast tea and toast.

'Excuse me,' she said, stepping out into the hallway to answer it.

'Join me for lunch,' Gio suggested. 'I'll send a car to pick you up—'

'Lunch? I only take an hour,' Leah said reluctantly, wanting to see him and yet not wanting to see him at one and the same time. Where Gio was concerned, she was in total conflict.

'My daughter's coming this afternoon,' Mrs Evans declared from the doorway. 'Take as long as you like. You've already done all sorts of things for me that weren't in your job description.'

Leah agreed to lunch, wondering what Gio wanted even while she wondered if she should have turned him down flat after his insinuation that the child she was carrying might not be his. Ari had counselled her to either take the DNA test or keep her distance from Gio until after she had had her child. It was sensible advice but taking that test would entail sacrificing what little remained of her pride. On her terms, it would mean a climbdown, an admission that possibly there *could* be some doubt about the paternity of her child, and she wasn't prepared to allow Gio Zanetti to believe that.

Why did that matter to her? Why did she care about his opinion? Particularly when she had had a one-night stand with him and flouted her own beliefs in not saving that first experience for a more meaningful relationship? Oliver had utterly destroyed her faith in meaningful relationships, she conceded ruefully, and even as Oliver's indifference had wrecked her pride, Gio's desire for her had finally made her feel like an attractive woman again. But how on earth could she have been such an idiot? So short-sighted? So careless of consequences? Why had she stopped taking the pill? But beating herself up for what could not be changed was pointless and what Gio thought of her was unimportant when she needed neither him nor his money in her life to survive.

But she did *need* him to be a father for her child, she acknowledged unhappily. She had grown up without a father and throughout her childhood she had longed to have a father the same as her friends. Little glimpses of other men with their daughters had made her envious and sad about what she had missed out on. Even so, would Gio even be willing to take on a paternal role? She supposed she wouldn't know until after her child was born and she supposed that then she would have no choice but to take a DNA test to put his doubts to rest.

She had conceived a child with a distrustful guy, she conceded with regret. He was unwilling to take anything on trust, much like herself, she conceded in surprise at that acknowledgement. Just as she found it hard to trust men, Gio was challenged to trust women. That reality made her a tiny bit more forgiving of his suspicions. Someone or a variety of someones had made Gio reluctant to trust as well. Gio would need proof that her child was his child too and, if she wanted him to bond with their baby and take on a father's role, she would have to provide him with that proof on paper.

And in the meantime, if she truly wanted Gio to be a father for their child's benefit, she needed to make him feel involved in her pregnancy, didn't she? She thought of the appointment with Cleo's obstetrician, which Cleo had made for her for the next day. She would have an ultrasound, Cleo had assured her. Hopefully, she would see the very first picture of her child and find out the sex. Feeling guilty that she had waited so long to have a proper medical examination, she decided simultaneously that she would offer Gio the chance to accompany her and share in the experience. If he said no, well, at least she would have done her best to include him.

Leah changed for her lunch date. Clothes were already refusing to fit her changing shape and she bit her lip in dismay as her best jeans refused to fasten at the waist. Her leggings and her older jeans were shabby and she refused to wear them. Even worse, her once slender waist had disappeared without her really noticing. She hadn't expected those changes to take place quite so quickly and she swallowed hard, knowing she had a shopping trip ahead of her and rustling back into her small wardrobe in search of something a little dressier. A floral maxi skirt with a stretchy waist was literally the only thing she owned that still fitted her. She teamed it with a rather loose white top that concealed the curve of her stomach and winced at her reflection. No make-up. She didn't want him to think she was getting tarted up for his benefit.

A limousine arrived to collect her and her brows vanished into her hairline as it drew up, reeking of money and privilege. She had been taken aback by her brother's limo and it hadn't occurred to her that Gio might use one as well. Of course, they were both very wealthy men. Ari, however, had made a point of reminding her that she didn't need Gio Zanetti for *anything* now, not for money or support, but she had privately thought that she didn't want to take such a combative stance with her child's father. Ari was offended on her behalf by Gio's refusal to accept her word. Leah was offended as well, only rather more willing, having conceded her own flaws, to give Gio a second chance…

This time she entered his apartment block with a firmer, more confident step, straightening her slight shoulders as she stepped into his extravagant penthouse. She was shown straight into a spectacular dining room with fabulous views of the city skyline. As she crossed the threshold, Gio appeared through another door and stilled to stare at her.

'I was keen to have a private meeting with you,' Gio drawled softly. 'Somewhere where we could talk without being overheard.'

His beautiful eyes shimmered and glittered like diamonds in his lean, hard-boned face and she stiffened, immediately recognising the unexpected leaping tension in the atmosphere.

'I suppose that's sensible,' Leah agreed as he pulled out a chair politely for her to sit down.

'Would you like a drink?' he enquired, watching her hitch her long skirt to cross her slender legs, noticing that the top she wore was slightly transparent and merely enhanced the full thrust of breasts cupped in pale lace. As his attention strayed to her luscious pink lips, the thrum of arousal kicked off and he averted his gaze, furious with himself for being so ridiculously susceptible. Didn't he ever learn the lesson that marriage had taught him? It was dangerous to allow himself to be vulnerable with *any* woman. Hadn't his mother taught him that from childhood as well?

'Juice or a soft drink,' Leah responded, striving to relax even in the face of the tension he emanated. Was he angry with her? Had something happened? She was travelling from her earlier calm towards edgy discomfiture, and she resented him for having that effect on her.

He nodded at the hovering manservant and a glass of chilled orange juice was brought and set in front of her. She felt ridiculously like a condemned prisoner, having a last wish granted as she sat there at the table while Gio remained upright beside the tall windows. It hurt too that she still recognised that his impossible good looks were matched by spectacular magnetism.

'What's wrong?' she asked, driven into speech by the pulsing silence.

'I have only one question to ask you and I expect an honest answer,' Gio decreed arrogantly, the planes of his lean bronzed profile forbidding in the strong light flooding the room. 'What is your relationship with Ari Stefanos? I have the right to know the truth on that score.'

Astonishment gripped Leah and her caramel eyes widened at the demand. How the heck did Gio know about her brother's recent arrival in her life? Her newly discovered ties with her brother and the inheritance that had come with it were a secret and she had no idea whether or not her half-brother had any intention of *ever* going public with their relationship. The night before, Ari had seemed pretty much mortified by his father's secret affair and second family, not to mention being rather ashamed of Christophe Stefanos' undeniable negligence as a parent. Those were not solely Leah's secrets to tell and she did not owe Gio Zanetti a truth that could cause embarrassment for her big brother.

'My relationship with Ari is none of your business,' she told Gio with composed cool.

'Of course, it's my business!' Gio fired back at her. 'Naturally I'm concerned if you are claiming that you are expecting my child when there is *obviously* another man in your life!'

'Oh, so your nasty suspicions have tipped over into actual fact now that you have apparently established that I really know *one* other man?' Leah rounded her caramel-brown eyes to accentuate her stab at how ridiculous that statement was. 'Do I have to move into a convent to convince you that you have been the *only* man in my life since I conceived?'

Angry colour flushed Gio's hard cheekbones. In the smouldering silence, the manservant reappeared carrying plates. As he uncorked a bottle of wine, Gio informed him gruffly that they would serve themselves and he withdrew again.

'I want an answer,' Gio repeated stubbornly as the door closed.

Leah shook out her napkin with a positive flourish as she lifted her chin, her dark eyes steady. 'You're not entitled to an answer. You're lucky that I was even willing to have lunch with you,' she pointed out, lifting her knife and fork and quite determined to eat the delicious salad on her plate. 'According to you, my claim that I'm carrying your child entitles you to some sort of medieval ownership of my entire person and my freedom. Don't you see how unreasonable an expectation that is?'

'All I asked was for clarification of your relationship with Stefanos, who enjoyed quite a raunchy reputation with women before his recent marriage.'

Leah wrinkled her nose with distaste at that unsought information about her big brother. 'I suggest you look at your own playboy reputation with women before you start throwing insults in Ari's direction—'

'You're not listening to me, are you?' Gio growled, well-nigh incredulous as he watched her continue to eat with apparent composure.

Leah ate quietly for a few moments while she pondered his words. 'You haven't yet said anything which I want to hear. When I met you, you seemed such a straightforward guy,' she confided wryly. 'But I was so *wrong* in that estimation because you're not at all like that. Under the surface, you have more turns and twists than a Gordian knot. You appear to be a womaniser who assumes all women are unprincipled, dishonest and unworthy of trust—'

'That is untrue!' Gio incised in a driven

undertone, incensed at that reading of his behaviour.

'From my experience it is totally true,' Leah asserted, crunching through her lettuce with gusto and pausing again to think. 'You invited me here for lunch simply to interrogate me. Even worse, you're demanding answers to questions that you have no right to ask. I'm not married to you. I'm not dating you. I owe you nothing more than the information I've already given you.'

'I am trying to establish a relationship with you—'

'No, you're not. You're accusing me of carrying on with a married man. I assure you that there is no affair, but if you want an explanation of my relationship with Ari, ask him to elucidate. Ironically, he advised me to stay *away* from you—'

'Did he indeed?' Gio slammed back at her rawly, his biting fury at that news illuminating his pale gaze.

'Just until the birth, when I will allow you to have your precious DNA test as proof.' Leah sighed. 'And it was good advice, but I sort of thought I could include you sooner, which just goes to show how naïve I was. I mean, I actually believed I had been invited to a genuine lunch today aimed at improving our tricky relationship.'

'How can it improve when you are determined not to answer my questions?' Gio framed grimly. 'And why are you suddenly trying to include me when you said you didn't need contact with me prior to the birth?'

Leah pushed away her plate and tossed down her napkin. She stood up with thoroughly exasperated dark eyes locked to his lean, darkly handsome face. 'I want my baby to have a father because I barely have a memory of my own. I was afraid that if I excluded you completely at this stage it could damage any potential bond you might develop with our child in the future. I *was* planning to tell you that I'm having an ultrasound screening tomorrow afternoon at Mr Grove's clinic on Harley Street, so that you could attend if you want to be involved. But I can see now that *that* was a very foolish idea,' she completed curtly as she paused only to grab her coat and bag and stalked back into the foyer.

'Leah!'

Leah spun round, her pink pouty mouth compressed into an impatient line, and all Gio wanted to do was chase that expression from her face and erase the lowering thought that he had contrived, once again, to disappoint her. *Per Dio*, since when had he tried to measure up to a woman's expectations when *she* was the one being unreasonable? After all, a simple test was all it would take to remove his doubts that her child was also *his* child. Where was the harm in a basic test?

'I'm sorry, but when I saw you in Stefanos' arms it looked distinctly dodgy,' Gio ground out defensively.

'Ah…that's right, he arrived just after you left and so you saw him.' Leah's delicate brows pleated in confusion. 'But you didn't see any kissing or anything like that,' she pointed out, frowning then before making the obvious deduction. 'You're a jealous toad, Gio.'

A flare of disconcerted colour ignited over his sculpted cheekbones. 'I am *not* jealous,' he derided incredulously.

'Well, keep telling yourself that if that works for you, but the anger, the suspicion and the interrogation suggest another story. You don't have the right to question me about who I have in my life,' Leah informed him with spirit. 'We are not a couple—'

'We could have been—'

'No…*this*…would have happened.' Leah moved her hand across her abdomen, indicating her pregnancy. 'And it's obvious to me that we would have ended up at each other's throats regardless—'

'I don't think so,' Gio argued, stalking towards her, tall, dark and resolute, his spectacular eyes fierce, making her back up against the wall behind her. 'The passion would have cancelled out our differences—'

'What p-passion?' she dared shakily, her throat tightening, her mouth running dry as he studied her with the incredible intensity that she associated only with him. He looked as though every brain cell in his handsome head were fully concentrated on her and for some reason that sheer intensity of his lit her up inside like a torch. No male had ever looked at her that way until him and it had a power over her that she couldn't comprehend.

She was running out of breath. An intoxicating tension held her still, her breasts stirring inside her bra as she sucked in oxygen, her nipples tightening into straining peaks while a hot liquidity welled at her feminine core.

'Tell me not to touch you,' Gio urged her in a driven undertone.

Why did he have to say that? Nobody had touched her since him. Those words only reminded her of how he had made her body sing and how much she longed to feel that way again. 'I can't do that,' she whispered.

'Why not?' he framed in a sexy purr, leaning over her, resting his hands against the wall on either side of her head, caging her in with his big muscular body. Dimly she could feel his body heat warming her.

'Because...because...' And Leah leant forward and let her hands slide between the parted edges of his jacket and smooth up over his hard muscled chest, the heat pulsing through her metamorphosing into an outright unbearable ache that made her lower limbs tremble. He was so warm and the familiar scent of him that close made her head swim as though she were intoxicated.

Long fingers tilted up her chin; metallic silver eyes inspected hers. 'Your pupils are huge—'

'Are they?' she muttered helplessly as she finally yanked her hands back from him, guilt infusing her at that weakness she couldn't suppress, that wicked and terrible need to *touch* him.

'You want me too,' he husked with a raw edge of confidence.

She stretched up on her tiptoes, small hands

reaching up to cup his face. 'We can't do this,' she told him firmly.

With a rough sound low in his throat, he turned his mouth into her palm and slid it down to press against the pulse point on her narrow wrist. As she shivered in reaction, she felt the hard, urgent thrust of his erection against her midriff.

'I've had a lot of cold showers since you went out of my life,' he told her roughly.

'I was barely *in* your life—'

'But you left your mark on me all the same,' he breathed rawly, reaching down to clasp her hips and lift her up against him. 'And nobody else will do.'

Leah stopped breathing altogether. That physical contact was everything she craved and yet everything she shouldn't allow herself to have. Frustration currenting through her, she let her knees clamp to his waist, and she kissed him, teasing along the edge of his full lower lip, nipping across the upper just as he had taught her that one unforgettable night. He had the most beautiful, perfect mouth she had ever tasted, and she wanted to feel it on hers with every breath in her body.

'Put me down before this gets out of hand,' she muttered tightly.

'I'm already out of hand…feeling reckless.' Gio growled that admission soft and low, bending his head to kiss a teasing, enervating line down over the sensitive slope between her neck and shoulder, awakening a tidal wave of response in her sensation-starved body. 'I want to take you into my bedroom and ravish you. *Madre di Dio*, is that even allowed in your condition?'

'Why wouldn't it be?' she heard herself say.

With a suppressed groan, Gio slowly, carefully lifted her more fully into his arms and carried her out of the hall and down the corridor to his bedroom. She weighed so little and yet he was insanely conscious of the swell of her stomach and of a quite inappropriate desire to shape it with his hands. She was pregnant, definitely pregnant, not lying on that score anyway. And it was *possible* that the baby was his, he reasoned, entirely possible. But it truly didn't matter whether the child was his or not at that moment because it was her whom he was burning up to possess.

'I wasn't jealous,' he breathed against her reddened lips as he laid her down on a big wide bed and flipped off her shoes.

'If you say so,' Leah mumbled, wondering how they had travelled at such insane speed from discord to passion and why that passion had overpowered her every misgiving and why now she felt crazily relaxed as if she was finally safe. Safe from what? From being alone? She wasn't alone any more. She had Ari and Cleo and her niece now, the family she had always craved. Only for some reason, that wasn't enough for her any more, she grasped dimly.

'It was just anger. You were racing off to be with him when I was there right in *front* of you,' Gio specified without hesitation.

'He offered me dinner—'

'I would've offered you dinner.'

His mercurial silver eyes held hers and heat washed through her as he shed his jacket, wrenched at his tie, all that very formal expensive tailoring of his discarded with disrespectful haste as he stripped. 'I felt challenged, not jealous. I don't share. I don't cheat.'

Leah veiled her gaze and tried not to smile. He was territorial, possessive even, though she had not given him that right. His bronzed chest bare, the rippling muscles of his abdomen taut and evident as he came down to her, he bent his dark head and kissed her with a hunger that raced through her in an incendiary wave of heat. Her fingers speared into his luxuriant black hair as he lifted her up to him and peeled off her top. Her bra fell away. He caught her breasts in his hands, savouring their swollen fullness with an appreciation in his intent gaze that she felt to her very toes, as though her body was his alone to worship and admire.

He rubbed his thumbs over the distended peaks and her breath caught in her throat, making her gasp, and then he lowered his mouth to the achingly sensitive tips and she was lost entirely to the wild surge of desire that ignited the blaze at her melting centre. He found her there, skating across the aroused bud beneath her knickers, making her spine arch and her body jerk as he slid aside the taut strip of fabric between her thighs and found the slick dampness of her arousal.

'*Madre di Dio*, I want you,' Gio growled as he rose over her to remove that last item of clothing.

And then he found the hot, damp, quivering heart of her with his mouth and his fingers and his tongue and she was lost, utterly lost for long moments of blissful sensation that surged through her in gathering waves until she reached a peak that threw her up and into timeless space where she fell apart with sheer pleasure and the lingering deep relief of satisfaction.

Her body still on a high from that overload of delightful feeling, she watched him don protection. She couldn't credit that she had chosen to be with him again but, in that instant, it didn't matter that there were differences between them, it only mattered that he was the father of her child and she craved him like an addictive drug.

He drove into her tender sheath with measured strength, stretching her with a slow burn of wildly electrifying sensation. Her excitement soared to an impossible high because she was ultra-sensitive to every lithe twist of his hips. Heart hammering, body clenching in agonising need, Leah hit another climax and it wiped her out for long timeless moments while she slumped limp and Gio struggled to catch his breath again, finally rolling over to release her from his weight and thrusting his tumbled hair off his brow with a sated groan.

'That was unbelievable,' he muttered unevenly. 'Unbelievably good.'

Leah experienced a painful moment of self-discovery. She wanted to turn time back and find herself leaving the building as she should have done. Should've, could've, would've, she mocked herself bitterly. Everybody had a weakness and evidently Gio Zanetti was hers, only, sadly, he was not a weakness she could afford and, just then, she loathed herself for not turning him down, for not pushing him away. Instead, she had surrendered to her own lust for him.

'You see we have the passion. That's really all we need,' Gio intoned.

Both Leah's hands clenched into tiny fists. He had never come closer to an assault than he was at that moment with her because he was making her taste the consequences of her own poor judgement. He still thought it was acceptable to question her morals and, by succumbing to his appeal, she had betrayed herself, playing into his desired image of her as a woman who treated sex casually. As Gio stalked into the bathroom, Leah was up off that bed within seconds and frantically getting back into her clothes. All that was on her mind was escape at the fastest rate possible. Bare minutes later she was leaving the building, flushed and tousled but too upset to be embarrassed and reminding herself that she could actually afford now to take a taxi.

When he returned to the bedroom, Gio was utterly taken aback to find Leah gone. What was it with her? She had sex and then she ran like a deer being hunted. The first time, well, he had kind of written that up to his having become her first lover. Foolishly he had ignored her insistence then that they could only have one night together. No woman had ever told him that before, so he could forgive his own disbelief. But when it happened a second time and she disappeared, it gave him real pause for thought. What had he done? What had he said? It was hard to escape the idea that in her estimation he did and said everything wrong, and that suspicion hit him like a punch squarely in his pride.

He did not treat women badly. He didn't lie to them, and he didn't cheat on them either. Yet Leah behaved as though he were the worst guy alive. He wondered dimly if it could have something to do with pregnancy hormones, but he knew absolutely nothing about pregnancy, only that he had a friend who had confided that his wife had become very highly strung after she conceived. So, he wasn't about to take offence, he assured himself, immediately ditching his angry annoyance. He would accept her departure like an adult…even if *she* wasn't behaving like an adult? Gio gritted his even white teeth, striving to make allowances when he had never before in his life made allowances for a woman. He liked Leah's chippy feistiness, he reminded himself, he just didn't like the fact that he never knew what she would do or say next. To his way of thinking, Leah, in comparison to all the women he had ever known, might as well have been an alien from another planet.

Leah attended her medical appointment alone the following day. Cleo had offered to accompany her, but Leah had politely demurred. She was a single parent-to-be, she reflected ruefully, and she needed to get used to doing stuff alone. She didn't want Ari and Cleo to start feeling that they were responsible for her in the way that Sally had. She would get through her pregnancy alone fine.

Buoyed up by that belief, Leah was shattered when Gio strolled into the plush waiting room at Mr Grove's clinic while she was waiting to be called for her ultrasound. She wanted to hiss, *What the heck are you doing here?* but it was impossible to do so when they were surrounded by people. It made her feel even worse that she was immediately relieved that she had gone shopping for maternity clothing that same morning and was at least respectably dressed.

Unhappily, Gio Zanetti was the ultimate cynosure of attention in the waiting room. He was sheathed in a tailored navy suit that had probably cost a fortune and that accentuated every line of his lean, strong, muscular physique. It shook her to recognise that his lean, dark features left her bereft of breath and that she was not the only woman present who reacted. Every eye turned and lingered on him as he sank fluidly into the empty seat beside her as though he had every right to be there. And it was all her own fault, she acknowledged, because she had told him where the appointment was and he must have phoned to ask for the time…

CHAPTER SIX

'WHAT THE HECK are you doing here?' Leah contrived to whisper-hiss at Gio in the corridor after the nurse came to fetch them through to the surgery.

Gio sent her a slanting smile that made her treacherous heart skip a beat. 'I realised that you were right. I don't want to miss this opportunity,' he asserted, grateful that she didn't know the story of his marriage.

Of course, absolutely no one *did* know that story apart from Gio and his ex-wife and there was a very good reason for that, Gio allowed grimly. Naturally he had no desire to admit what an idiot he had been at the age of twenty-one. He preferred to forget his marriage had ever happened and, since it had been a dire experience, he believed that few would blame him for that attitude. Only since Leah's arrival in his life and her pregnancy had he begun to appreciate that that disastrous marriage had marked him in ways he had not appreciated.

Leah had already been through a preliminary meeting with the doctor during which various tests had been run and she had been gently admonished for not seeking medical attention sooner. Now, rattled by Gio's unexpected appearance and wondering whether to be grateful or resentful for his presence, she lay down for the ultrasound, striving not to feel awkward as she tugged up her loose top and pushed down her maternity jeans to enable the technician to work, rubbing on the gel and then wielding the transducer wand. Gio infuriated her to the brink of screaming by getting into a technical chat about the equipment with the medics. Talk about a disinterested bystander!

And then the heartbeat sounded very loudly and Gio fell instantly silent.

'Is that the...?' Leah began uncertainly.

'And there is what Mr Grove suspected.' The technician pointed at the screen. 'There are two babies. Would you like to know the gender?'

Two? Leah gasped. 'Twins? They run in my family.'

'Twins,' the obstetrician confirmed cheerfully. 'Gender reveal or not?'

'Yes... I would like to know,' Leah whispered shakily.

'Fraternal twins. A little girl and a little boy.'

Just like her and her lost twin, Leah reflected painfully. Sadness tugged at her before she pushed it away to concentrate on the joy of the twins she was carrying. Their lives would be far different from the chaotic childhood she and her brother had experienced, she reminded herself more happily.

Gio was transfixed by the extraordinary 3D screen that showed the babies lying side by side, depicting two little faces. He had never seen anything like it before in his life. But then, he reminded himself doggedly, he had never seen an ultrasound screen before. But it had also not occurred to him that babies could look quite that cute. But then, he didn't think he had looked at many babies before either. Maybe they all looked like that. He blinked while the doctor informed Leah that she would have to take extra precautions as a twin pregnancy would be tougher on her than a singleton one. He experienced an extraordinary urge to scoop Leah up into his arms and take her straight back to his home and it utterly horrified him, putting to immediate flight the temptation to instantly accept that those images were *his* children. *Per amor di Dio*...what the hell was happening to him?

Still very much spooked by that impulse, Gio left the room with Leah in silence and then turned his head to glance down at her, belatedly registering that she had an expectant look in her big brown caramel eyes. 'Are you even thinking about getting that test to sort stuff out?' he enquired quietly, careful not to sound too demanding on that score.

Baulked of her every naïve hope of sharing her pregnancy with Gio, Leah was cut to the quick by that horribly dispassionate question. If that was all he had to say after seeing those wonderful images on screen, there was no hope left for him. She stamped down hard on her disillusionment and told herself that she had got exactly what she deserved for expecting *more* from Gio Zanetti. What she needed and their children would conceivably need in the future, he apparently didn't have to give, and that was, at its most basic, an *emotional* connection.

'No, I'm not thinking about taking that test,' Leah parried brightly with a determined smile. 'You're going to have to wait—'

'I'll take you home,' Gio announced on the street.

'Thanks, but I have someone to meet in half an hour,' Leah told him truthfully and, turning on her heel, she walked away, looking forward to meeting Cleo for coffee and sharing her news with someone who actually *cared*.

For a split second, sheer frustrated rage over that unhesitating rejection rolled through Gio. The reaction was like a violent rip tide and that unnerved him. The son of a vicious, brutal man, he had learned from adolescence to control his emotions. He had grown up in an abusive home with a father who often lost his temper and responded with his fists. That cautious attitude had bled over into a defensive control that kept any too strong feeling firmly at bay.

He did, however, register that he had got it wrong yet again with Leah and his sculpted jaw line clenched hard. He wished she came with an operating manual he could read and comprehend. He was a male of a technical bent and he liked instructions. Right now with Leah, he felt as if he were stumbling around trying to cope in daylight while he was blindfolded. He was starting to realise that throughout his life he had only ever enjoyed the most superficial of relationships and that belated awareness daunted him. But he could *learn*, he told himself grimly; he could be different if he worked hard enough at it. It wasn't as though he were stupid—indeed Gio enjoyed a genius level IQ, which was what had rescued him from the mean streets of a poor, remote Italian town.

Leah was a little teary-eyed with Cleo. Seeing her babies for the first time had been an intensely emotional moment and she had badly needed to share it with someone, only her children's father had, sadly, been the wrong someone. That closing question about the DNA test Gio had fixated on was the proverbial last straw for Leah. She told her delighted sister-in-law that as soon as it could be arranged, she would be delighted to join her newly discovered family in Greece. After all, Gio had made it painfully obvious that there was nothing to keep her in London...

It took Gio Zanetti almost four months to throw in the towel and admit defeat in his efforts to find Leah. He was a very stubborn man, but she had simply disappeared into thin air. Her former foster mother had confided that she would need Leah's permission to tell him where she was and, since that had not been forthcoming, it had told Gio all he needed to know about Leah's opinion of him. The detective agency he had hired had got nowhere trying to locate her and Gio had slowly come to believe that only someone as wealthy as he was himself could have made it possible for Leah to stage so complete a vanishing act. It was for that reason that Gio had finally bitten the bullet and arranged to meet Ari Stefanos.

Only if he *was* to learn that Stefanos was behind her disappearance, Gio reflected grimly, he was highly likely to slaughter the Greek where he stood. Gio had ploughed through weeks of serious concern over Leah's well-being. He had even gone to the police when Sally had first refused to tell him where Leah was. He had ultimately decided that Leah was almost certainly carrying *his* children because, clearly, Leah wanted nothing to do with him, socially, sexually or financially, so why would she have lied about who she had conceived her babies with? No other interpretation of her behaviour made sense. He thought of her composed response to his suspicion that she had had a past relationship with Stefanos and gritted his teeth. Whatever the relationship had been, it had obviously not amounted to much when Leah hadn't slept with the other man.

'Mr Stefanos will see you now...' The announcement broke into Gio's intense thoughts and knocked him back to reality.

'To what do I owe the honour?' Ari Stefanos enquired smoothly as he crossed his office and extended a lean hand in greeting.

And that fast, in the other man's decidedly constrained welcome, Gio recognised that he had been entirely correct in his misgivings about the Greek. He shook hands and said without any expression at all, 'Clearly, you know about Leah and I—'

'I do,' Ari confirmed.

'And you know where she is?'

'She's staying on the island of Spinos. But not so fast, Zanetti,' Ari countered with an edge of disrespect that made Gio's wide shoulders straighten into a rigid line, anger firing in his broad muscular chest. 'I have a proposition to put to you and I would like to outline that with you first and hear your answer before we go any further. I've ordered coffee—'

'Not for me, thanks,' Gio demurred curtly. 'What is the proposition? And what is your role in my personal relationship with Leah that you feel you have the right to—?'

'I'm her brother,' Ari declared boldly. 'Her

closest male relative and I wish to protect her from further harm and distress.'

Her...*brother*? Gio was astonished. That idea hadn't even occurred to him. Yet he had considered every other possible connection between them from the workplace to a friend of a friend. 'But you're an only child—'

'My father had a hidden second family. In Leah's current situation, I want you to marry her to protect her name and reputation. That may strike you as very old-fashioned but, in some fields, I *am* a very old-fashioned man. Your children should carry your surname and if you do not marry her, they will have mine. I am not asking you to make it a true marriage, but merely to go through the ceremony and part at some mutually agreeable point in the future—'

'*This* is what Leah wants?' Gio interrupted in disbelief.

'Leah doesn't even know we're meeting. Of course she doesn't know, and she would not welcome my interference, but I fully understand what will make her happy and a father for her twins will make her happy,' Ari informed him drily. 'Are you even willing to make that kind of commitment? I do have a small inducement to offer...the Castello

Zanetti became my property at the end of last month—'

The urge to knock Ari's teeth down his throat was growing mightily in Gio and both of his hands were slowly clenching into fists. 'How did you persuade the old man to sell to you?' he bit out rawly.

'I'm now a family man. Your lifestyle wasn't to his taste…any more than mine would have been prior to my marriage,' Ari pointed out drily. 'I don't want the property. I merely bought it as an—'

'Inducement,' Gio slotted in with cutting emphasis. 'I don't respond well to blackmail—'

'And I don't respond well to anyone disrespecting my sister,' Ari countered.

'I *didn't* disrespect her!' Gio ground out furiously, outraged at the manner in which he was being condemned when he *had* tried to reach an accommodation with Leah. Admittedly, he had failed in that goal, but he believed that he had been civil and restrained.

Who did Ari Stefanos think he was to try and move Gio and Leah around like pieces on his chess board? He wasn't for sale and Leah and her pregnancy were not a situation under Stefanos' control. Leah was very much Gio's business and he would decide what happened next, *not* her brother!

Leah stretched her toes in her shaded arbour overlooking the sea on her brother's estate and sighed as she slowly wakened. As her pregnancy advanced, she had discovered that she catnapped on a regular basis and now that she was only a few weeks from delivery, that tendency had increased. In her own opinion she was as large as a beached whale and her exhaustion was understandable, only she also knew she was living a life where she was spoiled rotten and waited on hand and foot, so she felt guilty. *Guilty* for lazing about and reading and chatting and eating, *guilty* for not having a job any more, *guilty* for spending the money she had never had before, *guilty* for missing Gio...

And there it was, the fly in her ointment, the shadow on her day, the secret tripwire in her brain...this shameless missing of a guy who had started out as a harmless one-night stand before transforming into the most stubborn, tactless, persistent and hatefully annoying man alive! When had she caught feelings again? After Oliver, she had promised herself that she wouldn't do that again, not at least until a long,

long time had gone by and her judgement had improved. But meeting Gio Zanetti had simply upended her life and then Ari had found her and everything had become so complicated that her head ached just trying to think about it. Stress was bad for her and the medics had warned her of the risks, so she breathed in slow and deep to calm herself lest her blood pressure start causing problems again.

While doing that she patted her stomach with a possessive soothing hand, thinking warmly of her babies, active little creatures according to the number of nights they had kept her awake with their squirming and fluttering movements. She was a little envious of Cleo, whose twin boys had already been safely born, two beautiful healthy children called Andreas and Nikolas. Their christening was to be held the following day and Ari and Cleo were flying in to join her that very evening. The island of Spinos was gloriously peaceful, or at least the Stefanos beach house was, she adjusted, thinking of the busy resort at the far end of the island and the equally bustling village nearby. Gradually she raised herself into a seated position and opened her eyes. Midway through reaching for a chilled drink from the cooler at her feet, she froze.

A yacht the size of the *Titanic* was now anchored out in the bay dominating all it surveyed. It was huge, one of those mega yachts she had read about in a magazine but never actually seen in reality, and that was saying something because when Ari was in residence they received some very wealthy visitors, who arrived in their own boats. *Virgo*, it was called, she thought with a frown, wondering why that name seemed vaguely familiar to her. While watching Ari's security men setting off in a motorboat to greet the new arrivals, she watched two other speedboats race from the yacht towards the shore. One veered off to greet Ari's security but the other continued towards the pier.

Leah rested back in the shade and lifted her book, only to blink in surprise a few minutes later when her brother's security chief approached in a beach buggy. She froze when he explained that Gio Zanetti was asking to see her.

'Er…yes, of course,' she heard herself choke out in sheer shock. Gio had arrived on the yacht? Refusing to see him struck her as being childish when she had been hiding away at her brother's home for so long.

Gio, *here* on the island. She could barely get

her head around that fact, straining her eyes to stare across at the pier on which a tall, well-built male stood gazing back. Well, the giant silhouette of her even in the distance would identify her, she thought unhappily. She had got even more pregnant and large since their last meeting. Legs feeling weak, she stayed sitting down, watching as the other man used his radio and Gio climbed into another buggy to be driven over to her.

'Would you like me to stay with you, Miss Stefanos?' the security chief enquired protectively.

'Thanks, Dmitri...but that won't be necessary,' Leah declared with a weak smile intended to reassure that Gio might be many things but he was not a threat to her safety... only her peace of mind, she acknowledged as the buggy drew closer and she glimpsed Gio's lean, hard-boned features.

He was still so beautiful that he took her breath away and it stunned her every time she saw him afresh. Yet he lacked that arrogant strut, that unmistakeable conceit that could characterise very good-looking individuals. She had watched every female head swivel, every gaze linger in that doctor's waiting room but she had also witnessed his lack of awareness. Now she saw Gio spring out of the buggy, all six foot plus of him, casually clad in khaki chinos and a black tee, and he looked absolutely breathtaking as she rose to greet him.

'No, sit down…don't let me disturb you,' Gio urged in his dark deep masculine drawl that sent tremors down her taut spine.

Leah's cheeks flamed because she was thinking that he probably thought that she resembled a barrel on spindly legs and looked likely to topple over. The filmy, shapeless white kaftan she wore had not been chosen to be flattering. It had been picked because it was light and comfy in the heat.

Gio, however, was thinking something else entirely. He was transfixed by his first sight of Leah in months. Black hair tumbled round her expressive little face and down her back in a river of glossy curls. With her creamy skin tinted a deeper shade and her huge honey eyes locked to him, she had the rich luminescent glow of a gold ingot in sunshine. The proud swell of her pregnant outline took him aback and he acknowledged that she was carrying part of him, *his* children, and that could only fill him with awe.

'You look incredible,' Gio intoned.

Leah rolled her eyes at him. 'Yeah,' she agreed mockingly.

Gio tensed. 'I wasn't joking—'

'Then say something I can accept. I'm as big as a house!' Leah pointed out tartly and sat down again just as one of the beach-house staff approached to offer refreshments. 'Please sit down and relax,' she added brittly, belatedly recalling her manners.

'I appreciate that stuff is tense between us right now,' Gio remarked.

Leah sighed. 'Understatement.'

'I want to change that,' Gio stated tautly. 'Those babies are mine as well.'

Leah's expressive eyes opened wide in wonderment and she stared back at him.

'I'm not stupid. I worked it out...*finally*. You don't want anything from me. You don't *need* anything from me, so why would you lie?' Gio framed grittily. 'But on another note, when did you change your surname to Stefanos?'

A huge grin lifted the tension from Leah's face. 'As soon as my brother asked me to consider it. I had no special attachment to my mother's name and being a Stefanos, being fully accepted by my brother in public and in private as a member of his family, means a huge amount to me,' she confided. 'I pretty much lost the family I started out with, so it's very important to value the relatives that I have left.'

Gio's brows pleated and he looked unexpectedly grave. 'I feel that way too but the only relatives I have left alive refuse to recognise me because of my father—'

'But why?' Leah cut in, genuinely curious about such an attitude.

Gio breathed in deep. 'He was the worst of the worst. A murderer, an abuser of women, a drug dealer. I can say nothing good about him even now that he's long dead—'

Leah was so hurt on his behalf that she leant across the space that separated them and grasped his hand in her tiny one. 'I'm so sorry. That is very sad and even harder for you to deal with,' she told him sympathetically.

Gio surveyed her anxious, compassionate expression with veiled amazement before he blinked and studied their linked hands. 'Well, if telling you the sordid story of my background wins me a hearing from you, I'll talk about it—'

'Don't you normally talk about it?'

'Why would I?' Gio had been knocked violently off his prepared script because the conversation had not gone in a direction he had foreseen.

'Because talking about that sort of stuff is good and it can help,' Leah remarked ruefully. 'My twin brother became a heroin addict. After my mother's death and our father's abandonment, he suffered from depression and anxiety. I can tell *you* that, but I can't tell Ari that. He feels guilty enough about his father's behaviour without knowing how severely our brother was affected by those losses. Unfortunately, Lucas wouldn't discuss those things when we were teenagers and I barely saw him after that age.'

'I didn't talk to anyone about my feelings or experiences either,' Gio admitted uneasily. 'Perhaps it's harder for men… I don't know. I just wanted to forget about it and move on. That struck me as the healthiest approach. Can we talk about us now?'

'But everything that happened to you when you were young is still influencing you,' Leah pointed out apologetically, already feeling that she understood so much more about him since he had told her about his father and confessed that he believed suppressing bad memories was wiser than acknowledging them and dealing with them in the present.

'I don't do the chest-baring stuff,' Gio told her stiffly.

Leah squeezed his hand and withdrew her own. 'That's absolutely fine as well...whatever you're comfortable with,' she muttered nervously, but feeling rejected that he couldn't talk openly in the way she needed him to, for no difference could ever be resolved without communication and, clearly, he wasn't willing to do it. That did not bode well for the future. 'So...er...*us*? But we aren't an *us*—'

And that fast they were back on track and Gio breathed easier again. 'I want there to be—'

'But how? I don't think you're much interested in the babies inside me,' Leah fielded with regret.

'I am.' Gio breathed in deep and slow. 'I got it wrong before. I kept on giving forth about the DNA test when you were probably hoping I'd say something about what I saw on the screen in that surgery—'

'How did you work that out?'

'By your reaction, your disappearance,' Gio parried stiffly, faint colour larding his spectacular cheekbones, his uneasiness pronounced. 'Obviously, I'd screwed up. I'm not good at the emotional things—'

'Let's not exaggerate. You don't do emotion at all,' Leah countered flatly.

'No, I felt it and I suppressed it because the whole experience with you reminded me of the last time I let emotion carry me away.' Gio gritted his teeth because discussing private matters was for him like stripping his skin off. 'And that sent my life off its rails for a couple of years…and it was *hell*—'

Leah was gripped by that confession. 'Oh?' she said encouragingly.

Gio didn't want to open up but some facts he knew he couldn't hide and had to share. There was no reason to share any more detail, he consoled himself. He sucked in another sustaining breath before forcing himself to continue. 'I fell in love with a woman and married her. Step by painful step I learned that everything she told me was a lie. I divorced her.'

And give Leah her due, meeting those lethal icy eyes of his and reading the shadows and pain still lingering there, she knew that he was sharing to the very best of his ability, every bitten-out word falling from his lips like a bullet. 'I can understand the harm that would do,' she admitted quietly just as the refreshments arrived.

Leah grasped her chilled fruit juice while

Gio tackled coffee, as indifferent as her brother was to the intense heat of mid-afternoon in Greece. 'Sally was a therapist before she retired and started the animal sanctuary. She helped me adjust to my past. That's one of the reasons why I said that I was very lucky to have her as a foster mum.'

Gio groaned out loud. 'Maybe you should send her my way… That was a joke!'

'I think for you it would be like tearing teeth out,' Leah said perceptively.

Gio sent her an amused and appreciative smile. 'You get me.'

'Probably for the first time,' she acknowledged truthfully, conceding that she had never considered that he too might have a troubled background, which continued to influence him far into adulthood.

Months after the event, she condemned him less for the lie he had utilised to conceal his true identity when they first met. He had come clean without being forced to do so. He had apologised. He had explained his behaviour. But Leah had refused to forgive because of her sensitive past history with Oliver, who had hurt her so badly. Regrettably, she had let that experience adversely influence her relationship with Gio. Who could tell what might have happened between them had she simply agreed to see him again and to allow their attraction to progress?

'I'm here on a mission,' Gio explained. 'I want you in my life and I want my children in my life as well. What do I have to do to achieve that?'

Leah stared back at him wide-eyed. 'My goodness, you get straight to the point—'

'*Sì*...that's who I am. Right now...' Gio swept a hand in the direction of the sprawling luxury beach house '...you're the fairy-tale princess in the Stefanos tower and I had to sail a yacht here to reach you because I wasn't sure a helicopter would get permission to land—'

'*Fairy-tale princess?*' Leah gasped.

'You know, the one with all the hair she had to let down for the prince to get her,' Gio extended in impatient explanation. 'I want you to be *my* princess...'

Leah was aghast at the wash of reactions within her that responded to those words. Excitement, hope, desire. Indeed, a great wave of emotions engulfed her. 'And what would that entail?'

Gio set down his coffee in haste, the cup rattling noisily on the saucer. To her astonishment he dropped down on one knee right there in front of her with a ring he set almost clumsily into her loose-fingered grasp. 'Marrying me. Becoming my wife and the mother of our son and daughter and *sharing* that with me, so that I can be the father my own father and your father refused to be.'

In shocked incomprehension at a development she had not once envisaged, Leah stared down at the magnificent ruby and diamond ring clutched between her fingers. 'But you don't love me,' she mumbled in weak rebuttal.

Gio studied her with intense pale blue eyes that glittered. He had never looked more handsome, with the clean-cut lines of his darkly handsome face enhanced by the sunshine. 'I don't think we *need* love to do this...'

And with that one revealing statement, Gio sent Leah from the height of anticipation and delight down into the dark drowning shallows again, where she felt more for a man than she felt she should.

CHAPTER SEVEN

'LET ME THINK this over,' Leah murmured tautly. 'I wasn't expecting this… I'm in shock, I think.'

'This can work. I can *make* it work,' Gio swore vehemently as she curled her fingers tightly round the beautiful ring, her clear gaze intent on him. 'We can create a loving home for our children together.'

'It's hard enough for couples in love to have a good marriage,' Leah reasoned tightly. 'And we wouldn't have that love even to start with—'

'But we've got the passion and the good intentions. We both want what's best for our children and we want to give them the chances and the stability that we missed out on—'

Leah was tense. He was keen to make the effort, she acknowledged, and unexpectedly serious about what was truly important in life. He had finally come clean with her about his background. He had been honest with her as well about the broken marriage that had soured him on trust, women and love. Was it masochistic of her to now want to know every gruesome detail about his first wife? The *only* woman he had ever loved? Simply human nature, she reckoned ruefully, and irrelevant to their current predicament. She very much wanted what Gio was offering: a father for her twins and a loving stable home. She could provide the home without his help, but she suspected that a caring father figure would be worth a great deal more to her children than she could calculate.

He was giving her a choice, a clear choice. Either she assumed the worst of him and embraced single parenthood or she took a risk on getting hurt and gave marriage a chance. Common sense suggested she go with the flow, but Leah was also uneasily conscious that she was already much more attached to Gio than she should be. And how would that play out in the very sensible but bloodless marital relationship he was suggesting? Her feelings created an inequality she could not deny but surely it was better to have tried than not to try at all, she reasoned ruefully. Trying to protect her own heart when it would deny her children a full-time father would be selfish.

'I… I suppose we should give it a try…at least,' Leah reasoned out loud, only to gasp as Gio dropped down on the seat beside her, plucked the ring from her and lifted her hand to thread the magnificent ring onto the correct finger. 'Gio! For goodness' sake!' she censured then.

'At least I've got enthusiasm to offer, which is more than I can say for you,' Gio riposted in a tone of reproach.

Studying her beautiful ruby ring, Leah flushed to the roots of her hair. 'You took me by surprise and I'm terrified of making a mistake—'

'And how do you think I feel the second time around?' Gio quipped, tugging her closer and losing patience when he failed in that ambition due to the siting of the parasol support. With a ground-out imprecation, he sprang upright and bent to scoop her bodily up into his arms, pausing with a belated frown to ask stiffly, 'Is this OK?'

Wildly disconcerted at finding herself in his arms and striving not to agonise over how much she must weigh in her current condition, for there was nothing slender about a woman

due to soon deliver twins, Leah looked up at
him with shaken eyes. Their sudden proximity
had knocked her even more off balance. 'De-
pends on what you're planning to do next—'

Gio quirked an ebony brow, an expression
of unholy amusement glittering in his eyes and
tugging at the corners of his handsome mouth.
'A kiss to celebrate our engagement?'

A faint little quiver rippled through Leah,
darting down into her pelvis and tightening
every muscle low in her belly. 'I suppose that
would be acceptable.'

Gio sat down again with a wicked grin. *Acceptable?*' he groaned with a shudder. 'Kill
me now.'

Her gaze colliding with those wolfish pale
blue eyes, her heartbeat stuttered, and her
mouth ran dry. 'When have you ever been *only*
acceptable?' she whispered shakily, struggling
to prevent her body from relaxing too obviously into the coiled virile heat of his lean,
powerful body.

'You tell me,' Gio urged.

'I like the ring,' she told him, her hands flying up to frame his sculpted cheekbones, slender fingers stroking down over the rough black
stubble beginning to darken his jawline. 'But
I don't feel engaged yet—'

Gio shifted her closer and the ache at her liquid core intensified as she felt the unmistakeable thrust of his erection. 'That's not a challenge I can meet in a public place…your brother's security team is watching us with binoculars. The lenses are glinting in the sun. Your brother's not my biggest fan and they know it—'

'Ari will feel different when he knows we're getting married,' Leah forecast, leaning closer, her breasts pushing against his broad chest as she twisted on his lap to fully align their mouths.

Gio rejoiced in the awareness that he would have taken Leah's brother by surprise, which of course had been exactly his intention. He took the initiative then, brushing, tasting, the tip of his tongue delving deep, sending an arrow of stabbing heat to the very heart of Leah and making her tremble. With a gruff sound breaking free of his throat, Gio stood up again and deposited her very carefully back on her seat. 'Definitely not the place,' he told her in a raw undertone of hunger. 'Join me on the yacht for dinner tonight—'

'I *can't*!' Leah confessed in dismay. 'Ari and Cleo are coming back with friends tonight for the christening tomorrow. I have to be here. You'd be welcome as well—'

Gio doubted that possibility when he had told her brother impolitely what he could do with the Castello Zanetti he had bought as an inducement. There was no denying that that unselfish act had cost Gio a pang when he had spent more than half of his life desperate to attain ownership of the only piece of history, family and heritage he was entitled to claim by blood and birth. But Gio *knew* he could not give way to blackmail or hope to hold onto his bride's respect if he grasped at the grubby offer of his mother's former family home. He had tossed that proposal back at the Greek, while knowing that he had every intention of proposing to Ari's sister and refusing to admit to the fact.

'I have a surprise for you on the yacht,' Gio admitted.

'Is this the equivalent of an invitation to see your etchings?' Leah teased with a glint of genuine amusement in her vivid dark eyes. 'The ring was enough of a surprise for one day.'

'I can't get this surprise out from beneath my bed,' Gio confided. 'Although he gets up on the bed in the middle of the night to sleep in comfort. He is the *weirdest* little animal.'

Her startled eyes rounded in disbelief. 'Spike? You've got Spike?' she exclaimed incredulously. 'But he was adopted! A family gave him a home before I moved out here. I was really disappointed, but I was just too late to make a claim on him.'

'Apparently, Spike fell foul of the family cat,' Gio confided. 'They returned him and I have been allowed, not, I stress, to adopt him...but to *foster* him to bring him out here to you. He's had all his jabs but I would hesitate to bring him ashore with your brother's guard dogs patrolling. I think they would traumatise him.'

'Oh, my goodness... Spike,' Leah sighed in a blissful whirl, happy tears stinging her eyes. 'Can we go right now?'

Gio guided her over to the buggy still sitting parked and helped her in. He was smiling. He had never had to seduce a woman onto his yacht before and it had also never occurred to him that he would sink to the level of using a dog as a means of persuasion. But he really didn't care, not when for once he had got it right with Leah.

Evidently alerted by his staff, Ari had phoned Leah before she'd even got into Gio's motorboat at the pier. She hovered next to it while she answered his questions. 'Yes, he's here and we're going to get married... I think sooner rather than later makes sense,' she told her disconcerted brother, who seemed understandably, she thought, stunned by her announcement. 'Maybe you think this is a little sudden—'

'No...no, I think it's...timely,' Ari selected warmly. 'You can get married on the island this week—'

'*This week*...are you crazy?' Leah gasped as Gio lifted her gently and lowered her down while the crewman held the bobbing boat steady.

'I'll get it organised,' Ari told her cheerfully and rang off.

'Ari wants us to get married on the island,' Leah told Gio with a frown, unsure how well that interference would be received.

'I would've preferred to make our own arrangements but that's acceptable,' Gio assured her. 'I can understand that your brother wants to host his sister's wedding.'

The noise of the outboard motor checked any further conversation. Leah's head was in a whirl. As the breeze blew her hair into a whipping spiral of curls, she put her hand up to restrain it and Gio shot her an amused smile as if to say that she was wasting her time. He was drop-dead gorgeous when he smiled and her heart speeded up. Excitement shimmied through her as he handed her up onto the yacht and ushered her into a lift. 'This is a very big and fancy boat,' Leah remarked and then, with a look of sudden comprehension, she exclaimed, '*Virgo* was the name of the app you designed that made you famous!'

'And very rich,' Gio conceded. 'I had money to burn, hence the yacht. I often live onboard and work though so it hasn't proven to be the youthful extravagance I once feared.'

They emerged into a corridor and moments later Gio swept her through double doors into a massive contemporary bedroom. He bent down to peer beneath the wide divan bed. 'He's still under there,' he groaned in disbelief.

'*Spike?*' Leah murmured uncertainly.

The little dog shot out of hiding like a rocket and crashed into her legs. Laughing, Leah sank down on the side of the bed to receive his enthusiastic welcome. When she lifted him he gambolled round the bed in mad excitement, finally throwing himself down by her side to loll with his tongue hanging out.

'You're a daft animal,' she told him fondly,

stroking his back and smothering a yawn that had crept up on her out of nowhere. 'Sorry, I'm so sleepy these days.'

'I was planning to offer you a tour of the yacht but that can wait. Would you like anything to eat?'

Her brows pleated as she realised that she was really hungry. 'Just a snack... I slept through lunch earlier. I don't sleep well at night and it catches up with me during the day.'

'I'll order something.'

'Thank you for reuniting me with Spike,' Leah murmured appreciatively. 'I can't believe, though, that Sally didn't tell me that his new home had fallen through—'

Gio laughed. 'He was chased out by the cat. He'll never live that down. I asked your foster mum not to mention that I had him until after I had arrived.'

'Neat,' Leah mumbled drowsily, studying him with heavy wondering eyes, committing his bronzed and beautiful lean features to memory. 'You played a blinder with Spike.'

'I play to win,' Gio murmured softly. 'But I'm not playing right now.'

Of course, he wasn't playing, Leah reflected ruefully. Gio was driven by a stubborn ruthless temperament that was very much goal-orientated. Right now, she and the twins she carried were his goal. But once they were actually married, would he retain the same enthusiasm?

A stewardess brought her a light meal and she ate it where she sat. Spike was removed to his 'exercise area' and then returned to her. Leah intended to go off and look for Gio, but a full tummy and growing exhaustion were overwhelming her. She lay back on the gloriously comfortable bed and stretched her toes, kicking off her sandals. She would close her eyes for just five minutes, she promised herself, and then knew no more.

Gio returned to keep Leah company and found her fast asleep, Spike dozing at her hip. Shadows lay like bruises below her eyes in the sunlight and he frowned, quietly slid her sandals off the bed and flung a throw over her. Beside her, her phone emanated an angry buzz and he scooped it up before it could disturb her, striding out to the corridor to answer it, grimacing when Ari Stefanos spoke.

'Leah's asleep. I'm not waking her up. Yes, I do understand that you're entertaining this evening,' he confirmed. 'Thank you for the invitation. Send her outfit out to the yacht and she can get ready here. I'll make sure we're in time for dinner.'

Gio rolled his eyes as Leah's brother grudgingly agreed to his suggestion. He would have to make more of an effort to overcome the hostility between him and Leah's sibling, he conceded ruefully. Whether he liked it or not, Ari was family, Leah's family. Unfortunately accepting and trusting such a connection was a challenge for Gio, who had never had a proper family and who, after his own childhood experience, was especially wary of relatives. Furthermore, Ari had already offended him, pulling the Castello Zanetti like a white rabbit out of a hat in an effort to persuade him into marrying Leah. For Leah's sake, however, he would have to get over his ire and forgive and forget…not something Gio was good at doing.

When Gio wakened Leah it was dark and she was disorientated, unable to credit that she could have slept so long in an unfamiliar place. 'Gosh, I was great company, wasn't I?' she groaned and then, seeing the time on her watch, she slid off the bed in dismay. 'For goodness' sake, I'm going to be late for dinner!'

'Your maid is here with your clothes to help you get ready,' Gio told her soothingly. 'You have plenty of time and I'm joining you for dinner.'

Belatedly, Leah noticed that he was wearing a dinner jacket and narrow black trousers, tall, dark and impossibly sophisticated, the tanned planes of his stunning face smooth and freshly shaven. By the time she was showered, had done her make-up and had donned the full-length aqua-coloured gown, which did a masterly job of concealing her pregnancy, she felt much better. Gio swiped the pale fringed pashmina lying on the bed and draped it round her narrow shoulders to keep her warm and she stared down at the ruby ring on her finger. Her future had form and focus now. She was going to make a success of their marriage, she promised herself fiercely. He had made a major effort to turn their relationship around and so would she.

A formal dinner was served in the big dining room. Fulsome congratulations were offered and although Leah could see the hints of dissonance between her brother and her future husband, she could also see that both of them were striving to overcome what appeared to be a mutual wariness. Two alpha males, she thought wryly as they stayed up for an after-dinner drink in Ari's study when his other guests had retired to bed for the night, alpha males knocking heads over nothing in particular.

'My legal reps are drawing up a prenuptial agreement,' Ari announced, startling her.

Leah frowned and winced. 'That's not necessary—'

'It is. You are a considerable heiress now that I have...shall we say made the disposition of my father's estate a little more fair to you and your sister?' Ari declared. 'Legal safeguards should be in place.'

'That's only sensible,' Gio chipped in, disconcerting her with his easy acceptance of such an agreement. 'I will alert my team to prepare for a meeting.'

As Gio took his leave, Leah accompanied him out onto the veranda that extended the length of the beach house. 'We don't need a prenup,' she told him awkwardly, afraid that Ari might have offended him with that request. 'I don't know what Ari was talking about when he mentioned our father's estate, but I'll find out.'

'I imagine he feels that you and your siblings were unfairly treated in his father's will and he wishes to redress that. That is between you and your brother. As for the prenup, it is my wish too that we have one in place,' Gio intoned gravely. 'I didn't think of that precaution before I married the first time and I lived to regret the oversight.'

Leah paled and her tummy twisted, consternation filling her. By the sound of it, his first wife had taken him to the cleaners, and he was keen to ensure that if they broke up she could not do the same.

Gio swung back to her, his broad shoulders rigid, his darkly handsome face tense as if the bad memories roused by the conversation had risen to the fore. 'I'm not trying to suggest that *you*—'

'Of course not,' she incised tonelessly, keen now to drop the subject.

'Such agreements deal with more than the disposition of money,' Gio murmured in explanation. 'Were we to separate, the agreement will also specify custody of our children and access to them.'

'What a comforting idea that is,' Leah countered tightly, and she walked back indoors, leaving him to depart without another word.

Gio was an inveterate pessimist, she reflected heavily. Did he think it so likely that they would fail to make a success of their marriage and break up? In her opinion that was absolutely the wrong frame of mind to get mar-

ried in and she had fled before she told him
so. After all, with a divorce under his belt, Gio
had to have a more cynical outlook than she
had and she couldn't hold his past against him.
She didn't want to lose him, not after she had
already lost so much of her family and, also,
after the pain of Oliver's rejection. She didn't
want to demand more and challenge Gio. In
fact, she was scared to do so. It wasn't a good
idea to rock the boat at this stage either, she
reasoned, particularly when he might receive
the impression that she was reluctant to sign a
prenuptial agreement.

Cleo urged her over to the laptop she already
had sitting open. 'Now we get to look at wedding dresses!' she carolled with enthusiasm.

In a daze at the speed of events, Leah allowed herself to be drawn into that challenge.
The next five days flew past. Gio attended the
christening of her baby nephews, Andreas and
Nikolas, before flying back to London for a
board meeting. Leah was frustrated by the fact
that they spent absolutely no time alone and
she was plunged straight into choosing bridal
options with Cleo, dealing with the wedding
planner and selecting a dress. She also had to
persuade Sally to make the trip to the island

alone because her sister, Pam, had been swept off on holiday by the new man in her life.

The day before the wedding, Leah flew with Ari to Athens where the legal meeting to settle the prenuptial agreement was being held. She was anxious about what demands Gio's team might make with regard to their unborn children and she wished she had had the chance to discuss those terms with Gio beforehand. The idea of discussing such serious and personal matters on the phone had made her cringe but the concept of discussing those same topics in front of a bunch of legal eagles made her shrink even more, so she had already briefed Ari's lawyers on what she felt she could accept and what she would question.

It was a most unpleasant shock to walk into the spacious office and register that one of the lawyers present was Oliver Bartley, her former boyfriend.

She froze in her tracks. *'Oliver?'* she said doubtingly, the blood draining from her cheeks leaving her pale as he rose from his chair with apparent alacrity, his good-looking face wreathed in smiles below his perfectly styled blond hair.

'Leah?' he questioned with unconvincing surprise. 'I didn't believe it could be you. You've changed your name.'

'Yes,' she conceded stiffly. 'If you're involved in this meeting, you'll want to withdraw.'

Oliver stiffened in dismay, clearly not having foreseen the possibility that she might make that request and annoyed by the threat of exclusion.

'You know this man?' Ari queried with a frown.

'He's my ex-boyfriend,' Leah admitted with a shrug. 'It wouldn't be appropriate for him to take part in this.'

Ari nodded slowly in agreement. Gio strolled in at that point and one of the lawyers on his team inclined his head to bring his client up to speed. Gio settled icy blue eyes on Oliver.

'May I have a word with you in private, Leah?' Oliver enquired smoothly.

'Let's not hold the meeting up,' Leah countered quietly, taking account of their audience, sooner than say that she could not think of a single thing they could have to discuss, considering that they had parted on such thoroughly nasty terms the year before. Not once had he attempted to contact her after the break-up, so he had not a leg to stand on when he suggested they might now want to talk.

Aware of Gio's burning scrutiny, Leah took her seat, nodding as Oliver's boss recognised her with a neat inclination of his head and a broad smile. She might have seemed composed, but she was shrinking with mortification inside herself because she could not look at Oliver without a sense of burning humiliation, not to mention an unwelcome recollection of the pain he had inflicted on her. He had used and abused her without apology or regret because it had suited him to do so.

As the meeting concluded, Gio closed his hand over hers to help her rise from her seat and murmured, 'We'll have to talk about Bartley.'

'I don't think so,' Leah responded, lifting her chin. 'My past is a closed book, much like your own.'

'But—'

A serene smile lifted Leah's lips. 'It's not on the table for discussion,' she said softly, and it felt good to hold back on Gio for a change, to say only what *she* felt comfortable saying at that moment.

Tension ignited in the air between them. She watched his beautiful stubborn mouth flatten at the corners. Somewhere down deep inside her as she clashed with those silvery icy eyes of his, her body clenched wickedly with piercing sexual awareness. Didn't matter where she was, who she was with or what was on her brain, Gio's raw sexuality engulfed her every time she got close. A flush on her cheeks, embarrassment claiming her at a time when she felt as though she should be more restrained in her responses, she turned away, relieved when her brother intervened and commented on how civilised negotiations relating to the agreement had been.

Leah stepped out of the office to be hailed by Oliver, who was hovering in the foyer. Her soft mouth down-curved. She really didn't want anything more to do with her ex but her pride refused to allow her to avoid him by hiding behind either Ari or Gio. Although she hated being confronted with him again and remained angry with him, in every other way she had moved on. The young and naïve girl she had been with Oliver had grown up fast.

'You didn't do my career any favours in there. Your brother is my firm's biggest account,' Oliver told her grimly. 'Couldn't you have pretended not to know me?'

'I don't owe you any favours,' Leah replied

drily. 'And your boss immediately recognised me, so pretending not to know you wouldn't have worked—'

'You should have told me that you were a Stefanos when we were together—'

'We were never together,' Leah parried, wrinkling her nose with distaste.

Oliver shifted a hand in the air and lowered his voice. 'That business with Celeste…that's all over and behind me. A temporary madness is all I can put *that* down to now. I'm grateful for your discretion.'

Leah discovered that she no longer cared who was in his bed and she made no comment. 'Goodbye, Oliver. All the best for the future.'

And with that, Leah moved back to join Ari, rather than Gio, who had settled glittering diamond-cutting eyes on her for the seeming sin of straying in another man's direction. He was so ridiculously possessive, she thought, although he would never admit it. But he *was*. Oliver was her past and Gio was her future. Why didn't he see that?

Gio wondered why Leah's familiarity with the self-satisfied blond lawyer annoyed him. And the answer came to him fast. Bartley was a man whom Leah had loved. She had gone white at the sight of him and had tried and signally failed to cover up how rattled she was by his appearance. Gio, on the other hand, might be about to marry Leah the next day but he was also the male Leah had cheerfully walked away from after a one-night stand and that was a poor beginning that Gio was unlikely to forget. Nor could he overlook the unlovely truth that had a pregnancy not resulted from their intimacy, she would never have agreed to become his wife. Leah had kept on walking away from him until he'd got that message loud and clear. For the first time with a woman, Gio felt as if he was the one fighting for a more secure relationship.

Gio had invited Ari, Cleo and Leah out to his yacht for dinner that evening.

'Are you cooking for us?' Leah teased before they flew out of Athens.

'No, I don't think your brother would wish to sit in the galley and keep me company while I sliced and diced,' Gio said with amusement. 'My chef will do the honours.'

And Leah cloaked her eyes and thought how right he was. Ari rarely stood on ceremony, but he wasn't given to informality. He had been raised in a very wealthy family and he acted accordingly. Cleo, however, was much more easy-going because like Gio and Leah, she had grown up with very little money.

'I won't be staying late.' Leah sighed. 'I need a good night's sleep before the wedding.'

'Of course,' Gio agreed.

A superb meal was served on exquisite porcelain out on the deck. Ari and Gio talked business until Cleo complained. Over drinks, Ari extended a large official envelope to Gio. 'Our wedding present to you and Leah,' he explained.

Gio tensed and began to open the envelope.

'It's the deeds for the Castello Zanetti,' Ari clarified.

Leah was shocked but Gio froze as if he had been blasted with ice.

'The Castello Zanetti?' Leah questioned Gio. 'Your mother's family home? The one that the current owner wouldn't sell to you?'

'Yes.' That single acknowledgement slipped quietly from Gio's lips as he looked at her brother with cool, narrowed eyes. 'This is by far *too* generous a gift.'

'You're marrying my sister and I'm happy about that,' her brother murmured smoothly. 'I had the good fortune to acquire the property at the perfect time. Let's say no more about it. It *is* your family home.'

There was a tension in the atmosphere that Leah couldn't quite understand. Evidently, Gio wasn't happy about accepting so extravagant a gift. Since he had once confessed to Leah that owning his mother's childhood home was a major ambition of his, she would have expected him to be stunned by Ari's purchase and much more excited, pleased and curious than he appeared to be. Yet Gio's eyes remained cool, his smile distinctly forced as he thanked Ari for his generosity and thoughtfulness and said all that was polite.

'I can't wait to see it!' Leah confessed.

'Perhaps you'll spend your honeymoon there,' Ari suggested.

'Perhaps…' Gio conceded calmly.

Leah almost succumbed to her curiosity and said something when they were alone for a couple of minutes before she stepped into the motorboat to return to the island. At the same time, it was their wedding in the morning and she was cautious, reluctant to tackle what, she sensed was a sensitive subject. She didn't want to make a mountain out of a molehill or give Gio the impression that she thought he had been ungrateful. Possibly he was genuinely embarrassed by so splendid a present or simply annoyed that her brother should have pried so deeply into his background and personal aspirations. Or, possibly he had wanted the thrill of purchasing that family house for himself. Was that the problem? The sticking point?

CHAPTER EIGHT

THE CONSTANT DRONE of helicopters in the sky kicked off Leah's wedding day. Guests were arriving at a steady rate, many of them flying into the resort at the other end of the island until it was time to head for the church.

Her dress was gently gathered under the bust with a lace bodice, a sweetheart neckline and a floaty chiffon skirt. The tight bodice and sleek empire line were tailored to take the focus off her prominent bump and for the first time in months she felt feminine and attractive rather than ferociously, strikingly pregnant with twins.

'You look a treat.' Sally sighed fondly. 'It's a very feminine dress…but you'll never stand those high heels for an entire day.'

'They're gorgeous though.' Leah extended the toe of a pale sequinned shoe with satisfaction. 'I'll take them off during the reception.'

Her niece, Lucy, removed her thumb from her mouth for long enough to touch a reverent finger to the flowing gown and sigh, 'Pretty.'

'Don't touch!' Cleo tugged her adopted daughter back in dismay.

'Don't worry,' Leah urged, smoothing Lucy's tumbled hair in a soothing gesture. 'She's fine.'

Sally anchored the ornate diamond tiara that Gio had sent over for Leah that very morning into her springy black curls. It could only outshine the delicate diamond drop earrings her brother had given her as an equally surprise gift. The trio of women descended the stairs where Ari awaited them.

'You look amazing,' Ari murmured with pride. 'Gio's a very lucky man.'

They left the house at a relaxed speed because it wasn't far to the big church above the village built a generation back by the Stefanos family.

Her heart in her mouth, Leah walked into the packed building on Ari's arm, her bouquet of flowers clutched tightly in her hand. She focused on Gio's tall, elegant silhouette at the altar and wondered who his best man was. She hurt for Gio, though, because he had not a single family member present to celebrate his marriage, and she marvelled at the hard-hearted grandparents who had rejected him for his father's sins. She decided that when she got the right moment she would ask him more about his mother's parents because life was too short for such cold, judgemental separations, she reflected. Perhaps they were terrible snobs who could not overlook his unfortunate beginnings, but Gio was *still* their blood.

She was ruefully amused by her passionate need to protect Gio from anyone who might hurt him. She was beginning to really care about him, to see both his strengths and his flaws, and she supposed that was the proof that she was starting to love him. And wasn't there a possibility that her love would enrich their marriage and make their connection a deeper one? Even though Gio could infuriate her at times, she only had to think of him persuading Sally to give him Spike and his tolerating Spike with all his eccentricities on his beautiful yacht and her heart simply squeezed tight inside her chest.

Hadn't he been hurt enough in life by his dysfunctional background and unhappy first marriage? She had seen those shadows in his eyes, had recognised that he had suffered and that he had learned to guard his heart to protect himself. But he would soon discover that their newborn children's very vulnerability would break through that shell: she was convinced of it.

'You look ravishing, *bella mia*,' Gio murmured as the priest began the ceremony.

Leah looked up at him and meshed with diamond-bright eyes fringed by lush black spiky lashes and her heart speeded up and her thoughts fell into oblivion. She watched the wedding ring threaded onto her finger and then slid on his, laughing when he had to help as the ring caught on his knuckle. And then it was done and they were married and she walked down the aisle again with his hand at her back and she was in a daze as they posed briefly for the photographer. They were wafted back to the house and the smooth service of the wedding caterers waiting to look after them and their guests. A flurry of introductions to Gio's friends followed.

After the wedding breakfast, a nagging ache in her lower back kept her seated when everyone else was on the floor and she blamed herself for standing around too long before the meal. Cleo joined her when she was freshening up and said approvingly, 'I don't think Gio had a single ex on his guest list.'

'Well, why would he have?' Leah asked in surprise.

A glass of wine in her hand and possibly a little merry, Cleo told her the tale of her own wedding when Ari had happily invited those ex-girlfriends of his who had remained friends. The women had seemingly only attended to make shrewish criticisms of the bride.

'I'm surprised that you didn't strangle him,' Leah remarked with a grimace as the two women found a secluded corner to sit in and watch the festivities. 'Look, I wanted to say something about the wedding gift, which Gio didn't look overjoyed to receive. I think Gio was so *shocked* that—'

Cleo giggled. 'Oh, I don't blame him. Ari *was* overstepping giving the *castello* as a wedding pressie. It was contentious after what had happened beforehand and he did put Gio in an awkward position—'

'What do you mean?' Leah prompted with a frown of comprehension. 'What happened beforehand?'

'Well, you know.' Cleo was slurring a little, clearly struggling to find the right words. 'Ari trying to use the *castello* as a bribe to persuade Gio to marry you… I mean, that wasn't a good idea, was it? It put Gio's back up and, obviously, he was coming here anyway the minute he found out where you were. That's the only reason he went to see Ari in the first place—he was desperate to find you.'

Those explanations fell like stones thrown into a tranquil pond. Listening in shock and disbelief, Leah mentally raced from zero stress to a heightened unbearable level of stress. Her brother had tried to bribe Gio into offering her marriage? That fast, the bottom fell out of Leah's world. Every illusion was shattered and her enjoyment of her beautiful wedding destroyed. How could her brother have dared to do such a thing? To lower her to that level? And how could Gio not have warned her?

'Oh, my goodness,' Cleo framed, her hand flying to her mouth in dismay as she realised what she had let drop. 'Ari's going to kill me!'

'I'll talk to them both when I get them alone…er, later,' Leah mumbled, espying Gio across the room where he was chatting to several men. The truth had knocked her right off her perch, she acknowledged wretchedly. She had been feeling happy, looking forward to the future, maybe she had even been feeling a tiny bit smug as she looked at Gio's beautiful dark angel face and started thinking of him as being *hers*.

Only, by the sound of it, Gio had never been hers, nor had he had any intention of marrying her until her brother had interfered. My word, she had to be stupid to have accepted Gio's sudden volte face. She had miraculously moved from being the pregnant woman whose word he didn't trust to the pregnant woman he believed was carrying his children and badly wanted to marry. How come she hadn't smelt a rat in that sudden transformation?

Once again, it seemed, she had fallen victim to her own poor judgement. She had seen what she wanted to see, discarded anything that hinted at a less positive angle and she had accepted Gio's every word as though each were solid golden proof of truth and honourable intentions. But, evidently, Gio had simply packaged up what he believed she wanted from him and handed it to her complete with a fabulous engagement ring. And who had put the idea of marriage into his head? Her own brother!

A flush on her cheeks, a rage locked in her heart and a tightness in her throat that made it difficult to swallow, Leah fixed a smile to her face as Gio extended his hand to her and drew her under his arm while he chatted. The evocative scent of him, the citrusy tang of some designer cologne overlaying clean, warm male made her stiffen because she was not in the mood to be that close to him or to once again be made viscerally aware of his sexual attraction.

'I need some fresh air,' Gio admitted, walking her out through one of the sets of doors open onto the veranda.

Leah sank down into a comfortable seat while Gio lounged back against the rail opposite her, his long, lean powerful legs splayed. 'You're flushed…are you too warm?'

'A little but it's cooler out here.' She sighed, connecting uneasily with diamond-bright eyes.

'Please don't be offended when I say that I can't wait to get back to the yacht,' Gio murmured wryly. 'I'm not naturally sociable by nature and I would like just to have you all to myself. I've barely seen you since the wedding craziness kicked off.'

She supposed that for him, second time around, all the palaver of a big wedding did strike him as excessive. 'What was your first wedding like?'

'A casual quick thing. We were students. It was a civil ceremony followed by a few friends celebrating together in a bar,' Gio proffered smoothly.

And by the sound of it, much more Gio's relaxed style, although that thought made Leah think that she wasn't really being fair to him. Some men didn't enjoy the fuss of a traditional wedding with all the bell and whistles. Unfortunately, she wasn't in the mood to be fair, she acknowledged. In fact up until the moment that Cleo had wrenched the scales from her eyes, Leah had been thoroughly enjoying her wedding. Her dress, her flowers, even the sparkly shoes that Sally had correctly forecast would be hurting her within hours. She flexed her bare toes, the shoes long since abandoned in favour of comfort. So what if her dress trailed a little? It wasn't as though she was likely to ever wear it again.

'Were you thinking of moving the yacht?' Leah asked tautly.

Gio laughed. 'Of course, I plan to take you sailing.'

Leah tensed. 'I don't want to leave Greece. I've been seeing a very good obstetrician in Athens and I want to stay within reach of him for the next few weeks. Twins often arrive early and I need a C-section.'

A faint flush lit his perfect cheekbones, his lashes, momentarily dipping like black velvet sweeps over his light eyes. 'I'm sorry, I didn't think of that. We'll stay in Greek waters,' he promised. 'We haven't even had the chance to discuss names for the babies.'

'I thought of naming our son after you.'

Gio winced. 'No, it was also my father's name and we shouldn't pass that heritage on to our son.'

'I would like Aurora for our daughter. It's pretty,' she said stiltedly. 'But we'll know better what suits them once they're here with us.'

Some guests were leaving and Cleo came out to warn them. Leah got up, wondering how she was still functioning when she felt stone dead inside herself. It was shock, she reckoned, she was still in shock from the major fault line that had appeared in her fairy-tale marriage. Gio had only proposed because her brother had urged him to do so, and he had accepted a bribe to do it. His family home, the Castello Zanetti, what else was that but a bribe neatly packaged as a wedding present? And how was she supposed to feel about being bartered off with a property dowry like some medieval bride?

'I'd like a word with you in private,' she told her brother on the way back to the party. 'And it would be helpful if you could bring my bridegroom with you and leave Cleo out of it.'

His brow indented but Leah didn't want to answer questions and didn't linger.

Ari caught her elbow to hold her back. 'My office in ten minutes...'

Leah rubbed her back where the tightening ache was intensifying and paused to speak to her former foster mum, Sally.

'Are you in pain?' the older woman asked with a frown.

'A little. It's my back. It's been a taxing day,' Leah pointed out. 'All of me is complaining—'

'Including those poor tortured feet,' Sally teased, casting a speaking glance down at the bare toes visible below the hem of her gown. 'Are you sure you're not going into labour?' she added worriedly.

'Do you think I wouldn't know?' Leah laughed. 'Of course, I'd know!'

Bracing herself, a cold glass of water clasped in one hand, Leah entered Ari's opulent office. She wouldn't have admitted it to anyone but she was not feeling well and she assumed the nausea and the occasional blurring of her vision meant that she had overdone it a bit. Gio was lounging back against Ari's desk with a drink in his hand, the very picture of relaxation. Clearly having spoken to his wife, Ari, however, was better prepared. He raised both his hands in a surrender movement and grimaced. 'I *know*. Don't say it... I messed up!' he groaned.

'What on earth possessed you?' Leah demanded shakily. 'To try and barter me off like some Dark Ages bride with a dowry?'

Her brother winced. 'It wasn't quite that bad—'

'No, it was worse!' Leah proclaimed. 'You went behind my back to interfere in my life—'

'I was trying to protect you and achieve what I believed would make you happy—'

'No, perhaps you were embarrassed at having an unwed pregnant sister in the family and you wanted me respectably married off,' Leah retorted crisply.

'That's not true,' Ari argued.

'Well, from where I'm standing, it looks like it's true,' Leah reasoned tautly. 'My parents weren't married and it didn't harm me—'

'That's a matter of opinion,' Ari flashed back. 'But it's also a debatable point because your father was already married to my mother—'

'These days women don't need to be married to have children—'

'I'm aware of that but I acted... I interfered if you *must* call it that...because I knew that you wanted a father for your babies. You told me that yourself—'

Leah lost colour and turned away, stiff with embarrassment at that lowering reminder. Even so, she recalled that late-night chat when she had told her brother how guilty she felt about not being able to provide her children with a father and how it had made her feel as though she were failing them as her own mother had failed her and her siblings. 'Yes, in an ideal world, I wanted a father for my kids, but that's not always possible or even desirable. Please tell me how a husband you tried to bribe into marrying me was going to help the situation.'

'But Ari *didn't* bribe me,' Gio incised calmly, entering the conversation for the first time, his cool silvery eyes intent on her furious face. 'He offered me the Castello Zanetti and I refused the proposition and walked away—'

'Only to get it anyway as a wedding present!' Leah fired back, unimpressed by that claim of innocence.

'That was *my* idea,' Ari interposed with a shake of his head. '*Thee mou*, Leah. I don't want the property. When Gio refused the deal what else was I supposed to do with his mother's family home other than give it to him?'

Leah dealt her brother an outraged glance.

'You're not getting the point, are you? And my point is that it was *wrong* to try and trade me off into marriage as though that were the only acceptable thing to do in my situation! The last thing I need now is an unwilling husband—'

'I didn't try to trade you off—' Ari protested.

'I'm *not* an unwilling husband,' Gio slotted in quietly, only to receive a burning look of condemnation from his bride that would have caused spontaneous combustion in a less tough male.

'But the idea of marrying me *didn't* occur to you until Ari tried to persuade and *guilt* you into it!' Leah condemned brittly, a nagging headache tightening round her brow. She lifted a hand to rub at the pain in her shoulder, blaming the joint pain on her awkward gait. Since her third trimester aches and pains had become the norm for her.

'I saw it as the practical solution to our plight. Only marriage met our mutual needs,' Gio commented tautly.

Ari winced. 'You need to up your game in the persuasion stakes.'

Leah felt as though she had been stabbed to the heart. Was that all their marriage meant to him? A businesslike bargain to raise their children together? That was so cold, so callous and unfeeling, utterly bereft of any promise of the warmth she felt that she needed to make their relationship a successful one. And yet she had already foolishly begun to believe that they were now sharing things that made their relationship much stronger.

'It doesn't matter. This marriage is over before it even begins!' Leah exclaimed, reacting to the physical discomfort she was in as much as the hurt that Gio had once again inflicted. If it didn't work, throw it away, her pride dictated in an effort to save face in an irreconcilable situation.

He didn't love her and he didn't want her as a wife. She had too much pride to settle for that kind of bloodless marriage and thanks to her inheritance she was a financially independent woman, who had no need to be kept by either her brother or husband.

'You're angry right now. Don't make drastic decisions in this mood,' Gio urged grittily, pale below his bronzed complexion at that sudden threat.

'I don't need either of you to survive!' Leah lashed back at them and headed for the door, perspiration breaking out on her skin.

As she reached the door, her vision blurred

and she tripped over her long skirts, tipping forward and landing up hard against the wood, clutching at the handle for support.

Gio scooped her up as she sagged. 'You need to rest and take a deep breath,' he told her worriedly, settling her down on a sofa.

'I'm not feeling well,' she admitted shakily as a clenching pain gripped her abdomen. 'Oh, no, I think I'm in labour!'

Later she had only a blurred recollection of being bundled out into a helicopter with Gio and Sally accompanying her. She was frightened, frightened that losing her temper so comprehensively had put her unborn children at risk. When they arrived at the hospital she was rushed in the doors as though she were an emergency and when she realised that the twins had to be delivered immediately for both her sake and theirs, she only then realised that she was playing a leading role in a genuine emergency.

Gio's ability to remain wonderfully calm grounded her as she was prepared for the surgery. When he finally reappeared by her side, gowned and masked, she was relieved by the steady pressure of his hand gripping hers. The lights above, the clicking monitors, the number of medical personnel surrounding them unnerved her a little. Gio chatted to her and the anaesthetist and she was grateful for the distraction that allowed her to get her breathing under control.

She felt pressure and then a jostling sensation before her little boy was delivered. He was brought to her all cleaned up for barely a minute before being carried off to an incubator.

'They're not quite happy with his breathing,' Gio explained. 'Seemingly, that's common with a premature baby.'

And then their daughter arrived, squalling, with a cap of black curly hair like her brother before she too was borne off. It was all over very quickly but Leah felt inadequate and bereft that neither of her babies could stay with her for even a little while. When she arrived in her private room, Gio was waiting for her, Sally having stepped out to give them some privacy. He was not quite as elegant as usual. Black stubble framed his strong jawline, accentuating his mobile mouth and carved cheekbones. Even though he was tousled with his tie loose and his shirt unbuttoned at his throat, Gio still contrived to look drop-dead gorgeous.

'Our children are beautiful. I've just been to see them again...' His dark deep drawl was raw-edged with emotion, his pale blue eyes glossy. 'Aurora is doing a little better than her brother, but the staff think there is no immediate cause for concern for him. Would you consider Luca as a name for our son? It's the name of the priest, Father Luca, the man who encouraged me most during my childhood and adolescence,' he confided tautly.

'Yes… Aurora and Luca. I would be happy with those names,' Leah conceded, studying him closely, shaken by the display of open emotion that he could neither hide nor control, while still struggling to accept that she was now a mother, simply sadly a mother who could not yet hold either of her children in her arms. 'Are you surprised by how you feel about them?'

'Stunned,' Gio confessed with a sudden flashing grin. 'But not in a bad way. I just didn't expect to feel this immediate sense of attachment to them.'

'They're going to be staying in hospital for a while,' Leah muttered, regret, disappointment and reluctant acceptance filling her as she realised that her babies would not be leaving medical care with her.

Gio stood by the door. 'I'm afraid so, but the doctors have every confidence that given time they will gain weight and thrive. Ari's already offered us the use of his city apartment for as long as we need it—'

Her brain felt a little fuzzy but then suddenly she recalled her final threatening words to Gio and she paled, her eyes flying wide. 'Us? I'm not sure we still have an "us",' she framed shakily.

Gio bent to rest his lean hands on the foot rail of the bed so that their eyes were level. His icy gaze was diamond bright with determination. 'You have to give me a chance to prove that this can work. So far, I haven't had that opportunity. You can't hold your brother's crazy attempt at bribery against me when I turned him down,' he told her squarely.

And on the most basic level, he *had* refused that proposition, yet somehow he had still ended up marrying her and magically acquiring the Castello Zanetti all the same, she acknowledged unhappily. Yet right now, with two vulnerable babies to worry about, weren't there more important matters to concentrate on? For the present they were better together, not distracted by arguments and separation, she reasoned.

'We'll talk about all that some other time when we're not so stressed,' Leah murmured, resting her head back on the pillow, exhausted simply from the weight of making that one decision. 'But you should get that DNA test sorted out, so that that's out of the way.'

'I wasn't still planning—'

'You wanted it. Let's not be precious about it now. I agree to the test being done,' Leah framed flatly.

CHAPTER NINE

THOSE FIRST WEEKS after the twins' birth were ever after a blur for Leah. Sally had to return home to the UK within days. Soon after that, Leah succumbed to an infection and was laid low for a week while at the hospital their son and daughter lurched forward one step then back another. Luca only gained weight slowly and, initially, he had feeding problems.

Leah saw very little of Gio. They talked on the phone, they met at the hospital when he was visiting the intensive care nursery to see the twins at the same time, but just as quickly he would be gone on business again. He maintained a punishing work schedule and slept in one of the guest rooms. Occasionally he joined her for breakfast or dinner and, while he was perfectly cordial, they talked about nothing other than their babies. She had no doubt whatsoever that he cared deeply for their children but had no idea how he truly felt about her or a painfully new marriage, which had never even got off the starting blocks. He had told her that he believed their marriage could work and said he wanted the opportunity to prove that to her, but so far he didn't seem to be bothering to try and prove anything to her.

Her reminder about the DNA test he had once demanded had annoyed rather than reassured him and she didn't understand why. She had needed to know that *he* knew beyond a shadow of doubt that he was Aurora and Luca's father but, afterwards, she had worried that mentioning the test again had been provocative and given in the wrong spirit at the ultimate wrong moment.

The first week that Aurora came home, Leah was run off her feet. If she wasn't feeding her daughter, she was trying to soothe her and, after several sleepless nights, Gio strode into the apartment to find her in tears, fatigue and a sense of being a failure as a mother weighing down on her.

'Let me take her now.' Gio sighed, scooping the baby from her with careful hands. 'Go to bed and sleep. I'm hiring a couple of nannies in the morning—'

'I don't need nannies,' Leah protested.

'You need rest and you need help. You have to get your own strength back. Your body's been through a lot these last few months and you're not looking after yourself,' Gio intoned grimly, scanning her bruised eyes and drawn cheeks. 'It's my job to look after all of you and, since Luca will be home with us soon as well, we need extra hands on board, at least until the twins are a little less demanding.'

'I—'

'Don't fight me on this, please,' Gio urged ruefully.

Exhaustion down to her very bones haltered Leah's ready tongue. She slept almost eighteen hours that night and by the following evening the first nanny had arrived, a pleasant girl who in no way made her feel less for not being able to cope alone.

Over breakfast, while covertly feeding Spike forbidden titbits below the table, a habit that had converted Spike into his devoted mealtime companion, Gio announced further changes. 'We're leaving for Italy as soon as Luca is released from hospital—'

'But we can't leave Athens,' Leah protested, nervous at the prospect of leaving behind the support network she had established there.

'Of course, we can. There is an excellent

hospital nearby with a suitably qualified specialist available for any health problems the children might develop. We'll have the nannies with us. We will also have a full staff at the *castello*. They were hired to get the household ready for our arrival. *This* is why I've been working so hard since the wedding, Leah,' Gio stressed, studying her with glittering resolve. 'So that I could finally take some time off to be with my family.'

His use of that word, 'family', cut through Leah's consternation and took the sharp edge off her anxieties. That he was making that effort, had indeed already made such elaborate plans to facilitate their move, touched her heart. The various health crises the twins had endured had made her reluctant to leave Athens, but she recognised that, with Luca's release, the emergency was now over and that it was selfish to expect Gio to stay in Greece.

'And there's no pressure on you, no pressure whatsoever,' Gio emphasised smoothly. 'Your brother did tell me that, basically, you didn't care how long our marriage lasted, only that it took place to legitimise our children—'

Gio breathed in deep and slow, having finally spilt the words that had been burning a hole in his gut ever since Ari Stefanos had voiced them. The last thing he could afford to do was make Leah feel cornered when he needed to show her that he could give her the time and space to find out for herself that their marriage could flourish.

'Ari talked a lot of rubbish, because it's not as though it was something we ever actually discussed!' Leah protested heatedly, pale in receipt of the explanation he was giving her for his casual, distant attitude. He was holding back with her.

Her brother had made it sound as though she would be content with an empty shell of a marriage and now Gio was wondering if that was true, if, indeed, she had only wanted a ring and his name and nothing more. No longer did she need to wonder why he didn't touch her, why he had made no move even to share a bedroom with her. He was following the wretched blueprint that Ari had given him, leaving it up to her to decide what she wanted.

'If you want more,' Gio murmured sibilantly, 'you'll have to tell me. Just as I wasn't an unwilling husband, I have no desire to make you an unwilling wife.'

If you want more... Leah had wanted more from the first moment she'd laid eyes on Gio Zanetti. A lot of women suffered from the same affliction when they saw him, from the nurses in the NICU, who had christened him 'Mr Gorgeous', to the heads that swivelled to get a closer look at his breathtaking features whenever he was in public. Deprived of him, she scrutinised online photos; she had an addiction now, an incurable addiction to Gio. Now, flushed to the roots of her hair, she glanced at him, scanning the cut-glass cheekbones, the carved jawline and the stunning pale eyes accentuated by lush black lashes, and her heart skipped a beat as though she were still an impressionable schoolgirl.

She wanted him, she wanted *more* as much as she wanted air to breathe, but she could no more imagine making an announcement of that fact to him than she could imagine flapping imaginary wings and flying away. She couldn't put herself out there to that extent, risking humiliation and rejection, because he had made no such announcement to encourage her, had he? She had put herself out on a limb with Oliver, had been the first to declare love, the first to seek greater intimacy, and in the end that naïve loving trust of hers had simply become another weapon to be wielded against her and increase her humiliation. And did she really want to take that huge risk anyway when she had already loved and lost so many people, from her parents to her beloved twin?

Maybe Gio already knew that he would be quite content with a shell of marriage, full access to their children and an easy pre-agreed exit when he tired of the arrangement as inevitably any highly sexed male would. But Leah didn't believe that she could detach herself from her emotions to that extent and the prospect of unrequited love only made her tummy sink like a stone...because she had already done that once and she was determined not to do it again.

Surrounded on all sides by a pine forest, the SUV travelled up a twisty steep road into the Italian hills.

'There it is...' Gio indicated the great stone frontage of the *castello* and its massive circular towers where it stood in a dominant position overlooking the wooded valley.

In awe, Leah stared. 'It's a *real* castle.'

'Fifteenth century. The first Zanetti was a soldier and he built the fortress. His son became a very successful merchant and by the next generation the Zanettis were loaning money to royalty and acquired a title in payment. As the family grew richer their influence and ambition grew and the house became the symbol of their success,' Gio explained.

'How do you know so much?'

'The old man who owned it was a cousin and he wrote an excellent book about the family history. It was fortunate that the property fell into his safe hands after my grandparents sold it. He restored it. I've spent the last decade buying back the original family paintings and the furniture that were auctioned off to finance that restoration.'

'I didn't realise that the last owner was related to you—'

Gio rolled his eyes. 'He refused to acknowledge the blood tie. Like my mother's parents, he was appalled by my father and kept me at a distance. When he told your brother and me that he would only sell the *castello* to a family man, he was denying the ugly truth of his prejudice,' Gio told her tautly.

And Leah wondered what it must have been like for Gio not only to be forced to grow up with a violent, criminal father but also to be punished as though he were of the same ilk even when he reached adulthood. 'That was wickedly unfair,' she whispered.

Gio shrugged a broad shoulder as their car turned up a leafy drive. 'That's life.'

'But even when your life has proved that you're a different man, why don't they recognise it?' she asked in a pained tone.

'Because some people believe that in the end bad blood will out,' Gio proffered bitterly. 'If I took an axe and murdered someone, many people would nod their heads in satisfaction and say, "Well, he's Giovanni Romano's son. What did you expect?"'

Her heart clenched at the idea of him having endured that bias since he was a child and at the confirmation that his mother's relatives had decided not to give him a chance either.

The SUV drove through a huge archway into a paved courtyard and the whole illusion of the castle that was a medieval fortress melted away as she registered that the towers and the massive walls were only a façade, loosely joined to the far more elaborate and elegant building hidden behind. A great double loggia with a roof spanned the courtyard, linking two wings with lines of windows.

'My word,' Leah remarked, clambering out of the car, feeling the summer heat warm her bare arms, her attention skipping over the beautiful displays of flowers in stone urns. 'It's more of a palace than a castle.'

'It *was* the Palazzo Zanetti for centuries but

my cousin reclaimed the original name and opened a museum of medieval weaponry in one of the towers.' A lean hand rested at the base of her spine. 'Let's go inside,' he urged.

'So, this very grand house is where your mother grew up,' Leah murmured, smiling at the older man waiting to greet them at the imposing front entrance.

'Yes, but my grandparents also own a country property outside Florence, which is where they moved when they sold up here. Allow me to introduce you to Jacobo, who is in charge of making everything under this roof run smoothly,' he interposed.

Nothing could have prepared Leah for the sheer magnificence of the *castello* and her eyes steadily widened in growing awe. A spectacular entrance hall with marble flooring was surrounded by room after room of indescribable splendour. Ornate ceilings, glorious colourful frescoes and gilded furniture abounded along with rich soft furnishings. 'Good heavens,' she exclaimed. 'I can understand why you believed the *castello* was far too generous a wedding gift.'

'I've put some very lucrative business deals your brother's way in recent weeks. I can now consider the debt settled,' Gio countered, surprising her. 'In any case, I don't like to admit it but, but for Ari, I *still* wouldn't own this place. My cousin was never going to agree to sell to me.'

'That's sad. Is this the first time you've seen this house?' she asked abruptly.

'No. My cousin held open days in the summer and I sneaked in once when he was in the middle of his grand restoration. I was fortunate not to be recognised.'

Leah found that even sadder and she reached out to clasp his arm and squeeze it in consolation. 'This is your home now. Enjoy it,' she urged soothingly.

'You're the only woman who has ever tried to comfort me,' Gio proclaimed, shaking his handsome head in wonderment as he directed her upstairs while grudgingly conceding that he had never actually shared so much of himself with any woman before Leah.

'That can't be true. What about your mother?'

'She didn't have a nurturing nature. She worshipped the ground my father walked on though, no matter what he did to either of us, no matter how many other women he had. I loved her but she didn't protect me or herself and she wouldn't leave him and save us both,' he divulged grimly. 'He came first with her…

always. Now enough about me. You've dragged my entire family history out of me, yet you still won't tell me about your ex-boyfriend.'

Leah winced. 'That's different. That story doesn't reflect well on me, while your background is not something you could have changed. So why did you want this castle?'

Gio was disconcerted by her admission about Oliver and he wondered what could possibly lie behind her discomfiture before he answered her question.

'All the miserable years I was growing up I could see this place up on the hill built by my ancestors. It made me feel proud at a time when I had nothing to be proud of. It wasn't its ties with my mother that attracted me, but that sense of history and of previous generations. I felt as though this place would give me a refreshing new focus in my life, while at the same time suppressing some of the shame about my father's criminal activities.'

Leah nodded understanding as Gio pushed open a door to show her the large, well-equipped room that had been prepared in advance for the twins. Loudly complaining, Luca was being slotted into his crib while the other nanny fed Aurora.

'Is there anything you didn't think of?' Leah

whispered, impressed to death by the meticulous arrangements that had been made as she scanned the nursery. She soothed her son by gently stroking his head and he gradually settled.

'I depend on you to tell me,' Gio said lightly, guiding her onward to continue the tour of the upper floor. 'Let me show you your room...'

Your room, Leah noted with a sinking heart. 'Where will you be?' she asked lightly.

'Haven't decided yet. There's a dozen bedrooms to choose from.' Gio pressed open a door at the head of the main landing. 'You're in here within easy reach of the nursery, which I know you prefer.'

Leah wandered uncertainly into another large room, adorned with gorgeous drapes and exquisite furniture. Her brain was in a whirl. Any hope of the marital relationship she had dreamt of and hoped to establish was retreating fast. They had been married over two months and he was still treating her like a maiden aunt, keen only to ensure her health and comfort. She glanced at Gio, marvelling at his detachment from her and his blistering confidence in the stance he had taken. Diamond-bright eyes connected with hers and she had an instant reaction, a clenching sensation spearing in her pelvis, her nipples tightening with the instantaneous shock of raw sexual attraction that she could not suppress.

Yet she felt as though she and Gio had grown so much closer in recent days, only it did not seem to be changing his approach to her.

'I turned the connecting bedroom into an en suite bathroom and dressing room,' he explained, throwing open another door for her inspection, and she wanted to scream at him and tell him that she didn't care even if an enchanted wood complete with unicorn awaited her over the threshold.

'I want more,' she heard herself say without any recollection of having decided to utter that sentence.

But there Gio stood, six feet five inches of vibrant masculine energy and an innate authority that made her feel ridiculously safe, as though nothing bad could happen in a world with him beside her.

'More...?' Gio queried, visibly taken aback by that abrupt announcement.

'You said I had to tell you, so I'm telling you!' Leah snapped, her voice taking on a shrill edge of mingled annoyance and embarrassment. '*I want more*. I don't want the separate bedrooms, the cool polite approach or the conversations that only relate to the twins.'

A blinding smile slowly slashed Gio's lean, dark features and it lit Leah up inside like a torch. He strode forward, reaching for her with both hands, drawing her close. 'I had to wait for you to make a decision,' he breathed in a raw undertone. 'That's been a challenge. I'm not patient. I'm not used to letting anyone else have control.'

'But why did *I* have to make that decision?' she asked shakily, the tension of the moment almost overwhelming her.

'Because you chose to walk away after our first night together and when we got together again during your pregnancy you walked away that time too,' Gio reminded her with dark-toned precision. 'I couldn't afford to take anything for granted in this marriage and I need more than your passive participation for the sake of the children.'

'I'm not a passive person,' Leah whispered unevenly.

Her breath caught in her throat as he backed her up against the wall with the stealth and grace of a panther stalking prey, only no prey, she thought ruefully, had ever been more willing to be caught than she was at that moment when she finally understood why he had put her on the spot. For the first time she saw their relationship from his side of the fence and, inside herself, she cringed. She had continually closed him out, shut him down, never giving an inch, never giving him the benefit of the doubt. Unfortunately, the loss of her brother and the father who had simply disappeared had contributed to her insecurity. And then, Oliver had destroyed her ability to trust and she had allowed the impact of that ultimately meaningless relationship to almost wreck her future.

'Prove it,' Gio urged, pulling her close, unashamed to let her feel the bold thrust of his erection.

Leah was done with prevaricating, making excuses for herself and hiding behind her pride. She let her fingers trail from his broad shoulders up into his black hair, tousling the silken strands that she had grasped in rapture many, many months earlier. A pulse of fierce anticipation beat between her clenched thighs, a wanting so powerful it consumed every thought and feeling.

'It's been too long,' she whispered.

'Way too long,' Gio husked feelingly against her soft lips before he parted them and crushed her mouth hungrily with his.

Her senses spun as he bent down, scooped her up and carried her over to the bed. In mid-air she kicked off her sandals, a glorious sense of freedom engulfing her because, for once, she was doing what she *wanted*, not what her zealous inner critic told her she should do. There was not an ounce of self-denial left in her entire thrumming body. 'And don't you ever call me passive again,' she told him in a warning hiss. 'You can blame my inhibitions on Oliver—'

'Oliver...?'

Leah rested silencing fingers against his beautiful mouth. 'Let's not talk about him today—maybe tomorrow,' she suggested.

'Sore subject?'

'Very much,' she confirmed with a shiver of remembrance, but for the first time grateful that it was all behind her and that she had met someone infinitely superior.

He extracted her from her sundress, his gaze raking over the scarlet silk bra and knickers he exposed and lingering with all-male appreciation. 'You look amazing,' Gio said gruffly.

'Well, I'm not quite pristine any more,' Leah pointed out, wanting to mention her defects to warn him ahead. 'I've got stretch marks now—'

'Makes you even sexier, the mother of my son and daughter and still shaped like a glorious hourglass I can't keep my hands off,' Gio intoned raggedly as he scored an appreciative fingertip over a brown swollen nipple showing through the lace bra and groaned out loud, abandoning restraint to tug down the cup and suck the straining bud into his mouth.

Sensation shot through her quivering length as he pushed her back on the pillows and employed his mouth and fingers on the pointed peaks. The hunger followed in a surge and pooled at the apex of her thighs, a hot, melting liquidity that made her dig her hips into the mattress. The bra got in the way and was swiftly removed while Leah divested Gio of the silk shirt that showed off his well-delineated abs. He scored a teasing fingertip across the damp triangle of silk stretched taut between her legs and her spine arched and she moaned because she was achingly sensitive there. The remainder of their clothing was scrapped in a mutual scramble of seething impatience.

Fully naked, they rediscovered each other with exploring hands and willing mouths.

'I've wanted you for so long,' Gio framed roughly, his touch contrastingly gentle as he dipped a finger between her wet folds, testing her readiness as she arched up to him with a sound of need that she could not suppress.

A savage groan escaped him as her change of position put them into even more intimate connection and he pressed her legs back and forged into her with bold, shuddering force. 'Don't let me hurt you,' he urged.

'I like forceful,' she whispered suggestively in his ear, her entire body clenching in delight round his fullness. 'I'm no delicate flower.'

Gio took her at her word, abandoning the careful approach, locking into the excitement that had ignited in both of them. He twisted his hips, grinning down at her wickedly when she uttered a little cry of appreciation and wrapped herself round him tightly, drawing him in deeper to enjoy the moment more. He was like a well-oiled machine, possessing her with potent energy and strength, setting off fireworks of sensation within her until at last she reached the pinnacle and jerked and cried out as a tide of sweet sensation swept over her.

'I'm not finished yet, *bella mia*,' he told her rawly, flipping her limp body over and urging her up onto her hands and knees. 'Is this OK?'

'Just be warned. It's *so* OK, you're not getting out of this bed for a month!' she teased breathlessly, her heart still hammering wildly with excitement. She was shaken by the sheer heady surge of passion and intoxicating pleasure engulfing her. And there was a glorious enervating flood of joy that she was finally with Gio again and one step closer to achieving the normal marriage she craved with him.

'Is that a promise?' Gio growled.

'If you're up to the challenge,' Leah gasped on the cusp of a moan as his pace quickened, her body tender and incredibly receptive. Sensation jolted her with exquisite reaction, propelling her to an even more intense second climax and an aftermath of drowning delight.

Lying flat on the bed, she whispered, 'I swear that I'm never moving again.'

'Well, I need you to conserve your energies for the month in bed you suggested to me,' Gio teased, flashing her a glittering look of heated possessiveness.

'Jacobo mentioned dinner,' she mumbled.

'We'll eat late. Everything's on our timing here. Go to sleep,' Gio advised, stretching out beside her in complete relaxation.

They ate a snack supper late in the evening and fed the twins together before returning to bed. Leah felt at peace for the first time in months. They were no longer at odds, no longer being polite and careful with every word.

Gio had even been generous enough to admit that he would never have been able to buy the Zanetti family home without her brother acting as a middleman. Taking into account Gio's own disastrous childhood, she marvelled at his gentle, loving care of the twins and it continued to trouble her deeply that even his grandparents had rejected him out of hand. She still had questions she wanted to ask him but did not want to tread too heavily on sensitive ground. Gio was still very uncomfortable talking about his mother and she suspected that she could be the only person he had ever discussed his wretched background with.

Breakfast was served in the shade of the rear terrace that overlooked the sunlit gardens behind the *castello*. Gio was smiling, relaxed. 'You never told me when you lost your mother,' Leah dared to say.

'My first year at university. My father had assaulted her and, of course, she wouldn't ever go for medical treatment when that happened lest he be arrested for assault. A broken rib pierced her lung and she died. I never saw him again after the funeral. The one bright moment was when he was finally tried and convicted for his crimes. He had so many enemies that he died within weeks of starting his prison sentence,' Gio imparted grimly.

'Did your grandparents attend your mother's funeral?'

'No. When they cut her out of their lives it was final. I finally met them when I was eighteen, soon after the funeral. I was a student studying nearby. I read in the newspaper about how they raised funds for a local museum and gallery and when they held a meeting I attended it...'

As his lean, strong features tensed, the cool distance of unease and annoyance entered his reflective gaze but that still couldn't conceal the shadows of pain. 'As soon as I identified myself, they turned away. There was no discussion, no explanation, *nothing*. That was that. They didn't want to know me.'

As they walked through the garden beyond the terrace, Leah thought angrily of a teenaged, vulnerable Gio approaching possibly the only civilised adults related to him and being rejected as so many had already rejected him and her heart clenched with hurt on his behalf. By all accounts, his lady mother had been as indifferent to the misery of his life as everyone else around him, yet his grandparents could have turned that around for him had they had the courage, the foresight and the strength to ignore his parentage. Had they ever regretted that negative response? Thought better of it? Wished they had, at least, given him a chance to show them who he was *before* they judged him unacceptable? Gio had taken his grandparents by surprise in a public place. Perhaps had they known beforehand and had there been privacy they might have reacted differently, Leah reflected sadly.

'My grandmother must miss her garden,' Gio remarked with a curl of his lip. 'She went to a great deal of trouble and expense to make a garden here because the only flat land was wooded and the woods were supposed to be conserved at all costs.'

'She broke the rules?'

'I would assume so, but then the woods here stretch for miles. The garden is a little overgrown. The gardeners haven't tamed it yet,' Gio commented.

'It's still very pretty,' Leah countered, fingering the velvety petal of a scarlet climbing rose as she strolled past, enjoying the drenching warmth of the sunlight. 'Have you ever considered going to see your grandparents and giving them another chance?'

'No!' Gio's derisive dismissal of that possibility was immediate, and she spun to look at him in dismay, noting the shuttered hardening of his darkly handsome features. 'That will never be on the cards.'

Her face hot from the sense that she had stumbled badly on a sensitive subject, Leah turned back to study the garden. She had moved too far too fast with him, she told herself soothingly, but she couldn't help feeling hurt that he had been so quick to shut her down just when she had believed that all his barriers were coming down.

'So... Oliver?' Gio prompted, making her tense even more. 'You promised.'

'I met him in a wine bar when I was out with friends. He was good-looking, successful. I was bowled over,' she admitted frankly, thinking that perhaps if she shared freely it would have the same effect on him. 'But from the start he professed keenness without carrying through and I should've smelt a rat when he sometimes didn't phone me for weeks. We had occasional dates in public places and the relationship didn't really take off until he took me to a legal dinner with his colleagues. He made quite a fuss of me in front of them, more than he made of me when we were alone—'

'He gave you mixed signals,' Gio gathered.

'Oh, very mixed. All over me one minute, ignoring me the next, but I was infatuated with him and I just worked harder to impress him. I thought initially that possibly I was competing with another girlfriend...if only I had retained that suspicion. It was a while before I noticed how critical Oliver was. He didn't like the way I dressed, or my accent or my interests and my cooking skills were definitely below his standards—'

An unexpected laugh was wrenched from Gio.

'You see, he wanted me to provide fancy dinners for his colleagues and I couldn't do it. I had to buy ready-made stuff and fake it. I started to change myself to try and please him...' Leah looked sad. 'I was a total pushover for a man like Oliver. He was very manipulative and of course I irritated him because he didn't ever like or want me for myself—'

Gio frowned. 'Then why was he seeing you? Was he gay? Was that what he was trying to hide?'

'No, he was having an affair with his boss's young trophy wife, the gorgeous Celeste, but I didn't find that out until *after* he dumped me,' Leah explained heavily. 'He ditched me by text when the scandal of my employer, Patrick Lundsworth, being arrested broke. I was inconsolable and after a couple of days I realised I had left my raincoat at his apartment and I had to return his key anyway, so I went over there, expecting him to be out at work—'

'And you found them together,' Gio guessed with a grimace. 'You must've been devastated.'

'Celeste laughed in my face. It was her idea that he get himself a girlfriend to act as a cover-up for their affair. But by then she wanted me out of the picture because she and her husband had separated and she was so proud of her power over Oliver,' Leah told him in an undertone. 'She even told me that she had made him promise not to have sex with me.'

'Well, at least she spared you that and he didn't get to use your body as well,' Gio breathed in a raw undertone. 'If I'd known what he'd done to you the day we signed the prenup, I'd have knocked his teeth down his throat!'

His partisanship lightened her humiliation at having to recount the story of Oliver's deception. 'He told me then that he's no longer with Celeste and I was surprised—'

'I imagine the excitement and the challenge went out of it once she was freely available.

Nor would being associated with the estranged wife of his superior have done him any favours,' Gio pointed out with innate practicality.

'You think strategically like Oliver,' Leah registered.

'But I would never have done what he did to you. It was callous to deceive you like that.'

It was strange how talking out loud about Oliver had made the entire episode seem infinitely less important and had lessened the sting of humiliation that had been inflicted. The insecurity of her childhood had made her crave love and stability. She had been all too willing to believe in Oliver. 'I was too young and inexperienced to realise that something was seriously lacking in his supposed attraction to me... I mean, he jumped back from me when I tried to touch him—'

'You're a beautiful woman. I imagine he was scared he wouldn't be able to withstand the temptation,' Gio countered with amusement. '*Dio mio*, I'm grateful that he didn't get to touch you...you've only ever been mine and I value that.'

Strong on equality, Leah lifted her chin. 'I would've valued you more if you'd been a virgin too,' she told him.

'Little chance of that after the home I grew up

in. I was never innocent in that way because I witnessed sex from an early age,' he admitted in disgust, closing his hand over hers as she mounted the shallow steps of a stone-pillared folly. 'I'll tell you about my marriage some other time. I still don't understand why you're so ashamed of Oliver's deception because it doesn't reflect badly on you at all. You're very straightforward. You wouldn't recognise double-dealing and insincerity until you'd first experienced it. Don't blame yourself for his lack of decency. Sooner or later, he'll get his just reward in life—'

Leah laughed. 'Do you really believe that?'

Gio grinned. 'I like to believe in natural justice.'

She shifted closer and stretched up to taste his mouth with her own. He tasted so good she leant into him, her breath catching in her throat, her heart hammering again on that surge of sexual hunger that only he awakened in her. 'So do I,' she murmured.

'But I imagine Oliver will be most grieved of all that he allowed the Stefanos heiress to slip through his clumsy hands,' Gio derided with satisfaction as he lowered his head and toyed with her lower lip, his words slurring a little. 'His face was a study as you walked away.'

'Do you want to go indoors?'

'Not particularly,' Gio confided, sinking

down on a stone bench and tugging her down
onto his lap, a lean hand travelling up a slender thigh to tug at her knickers. 'I'm very, very
adaptable to new experiences with my wife.'

'I'll draw up a bucket list,' Leah parried with
a breathy little giggle and a shiver of appreciation that lit her body up as though she were
on fire. 'How long have we got in Italy before
you start travelling again?'

'Three weeks and then there's a board meeting I need to put in an appearance at.'

A heady mixture of love and lust shimmied
through Leah at the prospect of having Gio all
to herself for that long. 'I hope you don't get
bored with us.'

'The one thing you never do is bore me,
bella mia,' he swore as he unzipped his chinos and rearranged her, bringing her down on
his engorged shaft and making her moan with
startled pleasure.

Afterwards, she lay in his arms, relieved that
they were able to confide in each other and feeling a sense of peace spreading through her. In
time, she was convinced, she would know everything there was to know about Gio Zanetti.

Almost three weeks later, Gio flopped back on
the picnic rug under the tree. 'I was a student

and I fell like a ton of bricks for Gabriella. I'd had a lot of sex, but I hadn't been in love before. I'd just created my first app, Virgo, and it had gone viral. Money was pouring in and, to be honest, at first, I didn't know what to do with it—'

Leah was thrilled that he was finally willing to talk about his first marriage to her. 'It must have been an exciting time.'

His lean dark features tensed. 'When Gabriella told me that she was pregnant, it never occurred to me to ask her to prove it. It never crossed my mind that a woman would lie about such a thing.'

'I can't imagine you being that trusting.' Leah sighed, running a hand slowly down over a muscled forearm.

Gio grimaced. 'I was twenty-one. I thought I knew it all and I married her the same week she told me she had conceived because all I could think about was that my father had never cared enough for my mother to marry her. I wanted to be there in every way for her and my child,' he confessed ruefully. 'Gabriella assumed she'd be able to fall pregnant *after* the wedding, but it didn't happen and eventually she got tired of the pretence and started drinking and going out again when I was working. There were rows. Some time after that she brought another man home and banged him and I walked in on it…'

'That was some wake-up call. I'm sorry,' Leah murmured, belatedly realising why he had wanted her to prove that her child was his to allay the fears and doubts that Gabriella's lies had bred in him. Belatedly, now that she understood the man she had married a little better, she appreciated that he hadn't told her about his marriage in any detail before because he was ashamed of how trusting he had been at twenty-one, and that saddened her.

'She came clean then. I'll give her that,' Gio told her grudgingly. 'She admitted that she'd thought I was a great financial bet for the future and that she had never been pregnant. The divorce took for ever and cost me a fortune because there had been no prenuptial contract. It left me bitter and distrustful and determined not to get seriously involved with a woman for a long time. Do you realise you're the first person I have ever told that story to?'

Leah rubbed her brow tenderly against his shoulder. 'I'm touched. But no wonder when I told you *I* was pregnant it pushed all your panic buttons.'

'I *didn't* panic,' Gio asserted, sitting up and pouring a fresh glass of wine.

Leah grinned. 'As far as you are capable you *panicked*,' she contradicted, sipping at her wine while Gio's wolfhounds tried to sniff out and chase Spike, who was hiding under a shrub.

As Spike emerged, he made a run for a stone bench and jumped on it to start madly barking. The wolfhounds careened back at speed and, accustomed to the terrier's excitable nature, flopped down on the ground beside the bench. Spike joined them, scrambling up onto Lupo to lie down on his big shaggy back. Gio's dogs treated Spike like a puppy and let him take all sorts of liberties.

The past three weeks had been full of new experiences for Leah and her dog. She had explored picturesque San Gimignano, lunched in Pisa and toured the gothic cathedral in Siena. Gio had very kindly encouraged her to play the tourist. She had enjoyed a picnic in the Chianti hills and toured the highly successful organic vineyard there, which Gio owned, and she had got sunburned on a charming boat trip along the beautiful coastline of the Cinque Terre. She had seen museums, old buildings, fabulous craft galleries and had revelled in incredible meals in wonderful restaurants. He had taken her around Florence on a motor-bike, showing her the places he had favoured as a student, and she had been silently, ridiculously jealous that Gabriella had shared his life back then.

Thinking about how much she loved Gio sometimes made her head spin because she knew how vulnerable her emotions made her. She hadn't told him that she loved him because she believed that if she didn't lay that guilt trip on him there was more chance that he would learn to love her in the future. He had been in love with his first wife when he'd married her and he was clever enough to eventually recover from that bad experience. Why shouldn't she be optimistic? Particularly when Gio was steadily becoming more open with her and sharing all his secrets?

After all, right now, Leah was incredibly happy and the twins were thriving and slowly falling into a routine as they began to sleep longer at night. To her surprise, Gio revelled in the ordinary family stuff and he gladly joined in with bathing their children, feeding them and taking them for walks in their pram. Of course, he enjoyed all that, she conceded. Never having had the benefit of a normal childhood for himself, he loved seeing the twins enjoying that security and the love and appreciation that went along with them.

Leah still longed, however, to give Gio the blood connection that his Zanetti grandparents had denied him and, pondering that thorny problem, she had decided to approach them for him because he was too proud to risk rejection a second time. She had searched online to discover their names and, since their palatial country home was occasionally open to the public, discovering their address had not been much of a challenge. And after a great deal of thought, she had printed a photo of the garden his grandmother had created and had written a letter, identifying herself, mentioning their great-grandchildren and asking to meet them at their home to tell them about Gio, the grandson they had refused to acknowledge. If they ignored the letter, she would have lost nothing by making the effort on her husband's behalf, she reasoned ruefully.

She was convinced that his grandparents' acceptance would mean a great deal to Gio. Whenever she mentioned the older couple, she saw the pain in Gio's eyes and, even though she knew he would probably be angry about her interference, she thought that if she could help in any way it was worth that risk.

A response to her letter awaited her back at the *castello* and she hid it in her sleeve before Gio could enquire about it because she didn't want to tell him any lies. She was shaken that she could have received a reply so soon and nervous in the sense that she had now started something that was no longer wholly in her control. Opening the letter in private, she found a formal reply inviting her to visit and giving her a phone number. She immediately decided to visit the elderly Zanettis while Gio was in the UK on business.

Gio's grandparents, Eufrasio and Matalia Zanetti, the Conte and Contessa Santastino, lived in a country house only marginally less imposing than the *castello* they had sold.

The week after that letter arrived, Leah stepped out of the car that had brought her to the house outside Florence and lifted her chin. Now she would discover whether or not Gio was correct in his conviction that the older couple were inveterate snobs obsessed with their pedigreed lineage and, even decades on, still painfully sensitive to their daughter's fall from grace.

What worried Leah most of all was the horrid suspicion that Gio would kill her if he knew where she was and what she was trying to do for him. They had grown so close and now she was doing something he probably would disapprove of and he might well be furious with her, she reasoned nervously. Gio, after all, had a great deal of pride. He didn't look back with regret to the past because he was too busy moving forward at speed. He didn't give those who wronged him a second chance, didn't believe in it but, even so, he had given Leah more than one chance, hadn't he? Had that only been because she was pregnant? His dreadful childhood and his resolve that he would make every possible effort to be a good and active father to his own offspring? Was the wedding ring on her finger only there for those most basic reasons?

She was probably kidding herself if she allowed herself to believe that she was anything more important to Gio than the mother of his children, the wife he required to create a secure traditional home for the twins. He made her happy and he seemed happy with her, but he had told her from the start that he wasn't offering her love, so she couldn't say she was being short-changed, could she?

Sadly, when she had told Gio that she wanted

more she had truly meant that she wanted a great deal more than his wildly entertaining expertise between the sheets.

Admittedly, he was incredible in bed, she thought, her cheeks warming at the reflection that Gio had needed to go away for a night or two to allow her to catch up on her sleep. And it was not as though intimacy were confined only to the night hours. Once Gio had registered that Leah was fascinated by encounters in unexpected places, he had ensured that he delivered on that score as well. Their only disappointment had been making love in the Maserati when they had ended up getting out of the car and using the bonnet instead, but by that stage of the proceedings Leah had been so consumed by giggles that Gio had marvelled at his ability to save the day.

Her body still heated by her recollection of that episode, Leah entered the classy drawing room of the Conte and Contessa's home with a straight back and a composed expression. Dealing with guests by Ari and Cleo's side had given her a great deal more social confidence than she had once had but facing up to Gio's blood relatives still demanded considerable courage. Although they were now in their late seventies, his grandparents were elegantly dressed and still upright and strong.

'Please sit down, Leah. We do appreciate your visit,' Gio's grandmother said in accented English.

'Hopefully you are not as hot-headed as the man you married,' her husband remarked, provoking his wife into a staccato burst of Italian.

'You see how hen-pecked I am,' he lamented with a glint of amusement in his creased eyes.

'You're not hen-pecked, you're grumpy because you haven't had your afternoon tea yet,' his wife told him roundly, pressing a bell by the fireplace.

Moments later a maid came in carrying a tray and a very formal afternoon tea session commenced, complete with bone-thin porcelain, cloth napkins, minuscule sandwiches, even tinier fancy cakes and solid silver cutlery. Leah was grateful that Gio wasn't with her. His tolerance threshold for extreme formality and exaggerated old-style courtesies was low. While her brother was very much at home with such customs, Gio, denied such experiences when he was younger, was aggressively contemporary in his habits.

'At that first meeting with him at the museum we weren't prepared and we didn't know what to say. One moment he was there and then he stomped off and that was that,' the older woman explained heavily.

'I was concerned to see that he had the hot temper his father was famed for,' her husband added.

'Gio doesn't lose his temper,' Leah responded carefully. 'He's very controlled, very cautious. I think his background made him that way.'

'It doesn't help that he's the very picture of his father,' Gio's grandfather admitted, compressing his lips. 'But it was unreasonable to judge him for that.'

'His father *was* a vile character,' Matalia Zanetti murmured tightly. 'We did everything within our power to try and persuade our daughter to leave him, but she was as addicted to him as some were to the drugs he sold. Nothing would move her and in the end we had to accept that she was where she wanted to be.'

'The town priest, Father Luca, came to us when Gio was a boy and told us that he was being neglected and he asked us to consider fighting for custody.'

The old man looked very sad. 'We felt we could not face another scandal in the newspapers and the dragging out of all that dirt concerning our daughter again. We also thought the priest was exaggerating but stories came out after Gio's father's imprisonment and subsequent death which horrified us. We let Gio down badly and from what we read about him, he deserved so much more from us.'

'But by then it was too late and Gio had come to Florence as a student and we had simply stared dumbly at him as though he were an exotic beast when he approached us.' Gio's grandmother's eyes were bright with unshed tears, her deep sigh one of regret.

'Well, all that's behind you now,' Leah pointed out, keen to inject a more positive note into the conversation but suddenly very pleased that she had taken the risk of visiting on Gio's behalf. 'I'm suggesting a fresh start and staying away from the past because everybody is sure to have a different opinion on that. Gio loathed his father, but he wasn't close to his mother either because she didn't ever try to protect him from his father. It's better for you to know that in advance.'

'You're a very sensible young woman,' the Contessa told her. 'How do you suggest we go about meeting our grandson?'

'We're holding the twins' christening in the *castello* chapel in ten days. That gives me plenty of time to explain to Gio that I visited you. I brought an invitation for you,' Leah admitted, digging into her capacious leather bag to extend it.

'Do you have any pictures of the twins…? Oh, yes, I have kept up with the news,' Gio's grandmother admitted with a smile.

Smiling back, Leah extended her phone and brought up the most recent photos. There was one of Gio holding Aurora and she noticed his grandparents lingered over that one the longest. 'He's a wonderful man,' she said quietly. 'Very clever, generous and caring. I think the only lessons he learned from his father were how not to be like him.'

'Your love for him shines in your eyes,' the Contessa said softly.

Leah was in the best of good moods and feeling sentimental when the limousine delivered her home to the *castello*. She walked in the front door held wide by a curiously tense Jacobo and glanced up with a smile as Gio stalked into the hall.

'My goodness, I wasn't expecting you back until tomorrow,' she told him chirpily.

'Was that why you felt confident enough to believe that I wouldn't realise that you'd betrayed my trust?'

CHAPTER TEN

AND, THAT FAST, Leah knew that somehow Gio also knew where she had been and her tummy sank like a stone to her very toes. 'How did you find out where I was?' she almost whispered, horror gripping her when she collided with the biting, stinging chill of his glittering wolfish gaze.

In all their relationship, Gio had never looked at her like that: with raging hostility, fierce condemnation and an even more terrifying coldness. It suggested that in his eyes she had put herself beyond the pale and done something absolutely unforgivable. Her tummy twisted, sudden pallor now stamping her taut features.

'It wasn't difficult. You hadn't bothered to cover your tracks because you didn't know I'd be arriving back early. I wanted to surprise you.' Gio visibly gritted his even white teeth at that recollection. '*Dio mio*, didn't that turn out well? Almost as well as when I decided to surprise Gabriella. I don't learn, do I?'

'Gio,' she began breathlessly.

'I called your driver to ask where you were. In the future if you're trying to hide something, you need to bribe your driver,' Gio warned her flatly.

And it was only at that moment that she truly understood how very shaken up and upset he was underneath that cold front of control. He was, after all, standing in the hall loudly saying private things where anyone might have overheard them, but she rather suspected Jacobo had guessed that trouble was in the air and he had quietly removed himself and every other staff member from the vicinity.

'Come into the drawing room.' Leah's voice was almost a whisper because tension had stolen the breath from her lungs.

'Oh, you've definitely been visiting the *grand*parents,' Gio derided. 'This is a living room.'

In a daze, caught unprepared as she had been, that statement of reverse snobbery made her spread her gaze round the confines of the vast opulent room, with its huge wooden carved hearth bearing the Zanetti coat of arms, ornate tall ceiling and decorative drapes. 'No, it won't ever be a living room unless you de-construct it. It's a drawing room because it was made like this to impress and intimidate visi-tors. Ordinary people don't have spaces like this in their homes,' she told him as though they were having a perfectly normal dialogue instead of a heart-wrenching fight that was tearing her apart inside herself.

That Gio could be hurt and angry enough to compare her to his ex-wife, who had lied about her pregnancy and slept with another man, appalled her. 'I would have told you that I was planning to visit your grandparents, but I didn't want to do it until I'd met them and sussed them out… I didn't want them upsetting you in some way,' she admitted doggedly, de-termined to explain her reasoning. 'I was sort of vetting them for you in advance.'

'Naturally, it wouldn't have occurred to you that, ironically just like them, I had a cer-tain prejudiced reason to keep my distance?' Gio raised an ebony brow enquiringly. 'They brought up my mother and she was a sociopath who didn't have a single drop of love or com-passion in her heart, even for her child. Why would I seek them out now that I am no lon-ger vulnerable enough to actually need them?'

Leah bit her tongue, unwilling to get into such a discussion when it was for him and his grandparents to bridge all the unmentionable things that had happened to him. She didn't think his mother's parents would be that surprised to find out how she had treated him. She had noticed that they had not uttered a word in their daughter's defence and had not referred to her as a victim either. 'Perfectly normal, decent people end up raising sociopaths. It's not their fault any more than it's yours that your parents were...unpleasant—'

'*Grazie mille* for that vote of confidence,' Gio mocked that understatement. 'But it doesn't excuse your betrayal in any way.'

Leah thrust the door shut behind her and protested, 'I didn't betray you... I would *never* betray you, Gio!'

'But you did,' Gio threw back at her with icy bitter precision. 'You betrayed me the instant you went behind my back to see my grandparents without my knowledge. I trusted you, Leah. Do you know how long it's been since I trusted a woman?' he demanded. 'I trusted you with all my secrets and you deceived me today.'

Leah lifted her head high. 'No, that's not

how it was. There was no betrayal of trust involved—'

'How can there not have been when you went to see *them*?' Gio accused with wrathful emphasis. 'You didn't even mention what you were thinking about doing and you didn't discuss it with me—'

'How the heck could I discuss it with you when you're not rational about it?' Leah slammed back at him, her own temper finally sparking in self-defence. 'You lit up like a firework whenever I tried to talk about them!'

'And you're surprised? After the rejection I had from them?' he parried rawly.

'No, I thought about that. You were young, Gio...you didn't think it through...approaching them when other people were around and without warning. They got it wrong and they *know* they got it wrong that day—'

'It's best that they remain in the past alongside my late parents,' Gio opined curtly.

'I assure you that I didn't share anything you've ever told me about either of your parents with them. I didn't spill any secrets and neither did they. That wasn't my business and I knew that. I only said that you were a wonderful guy—'

'You expect me to believe that?' Gio raked

back at her. 'You positively bounced back into this house looking very pleased with yourself. So, I assume your visit to them went well on your terms. It won't get you anywhere because I want nothing to do with them. So, why did you do it?'

'I—'

'I noticed that your brother was somewhat impressed by the fact that my grandparents were titled,' Gio continued harshly. 'And they do have an elite standing in social circles. Is that kind of social status and acceptance so important to you that you would rate that higher than my wishes and needs?'

Leah was utterly savaged by such a suspicion. Did he know so little about her? How could he even suspect her of such superficiality?

'I went to see them for your benefit. I told them nothing private—'

'How was it for *my* benefit when I've done without them all my life?' Gio flung at her in scornful condemnation of that statement.

'They're your family and I think it would do you good to have family other than me and the twins,' Leah declared clumsily, her eyes stinging with tears because that was not something he would easily hear or something that she had wished to be forced into saying. 'I know how much Ari finding me meant to me…discovering my brother was a *huge* thing for me and wonderful! I know you're probably not Ari's greatest fan, but the knowledge that he searched for me because I was his half-sister meant the world to me.'

'Ari *searched* for you. My grandparents always knew where I was,' Gio responded deflatingly. 'You can't compare the situations. But you do know me well enough to know that taking it upon yourself to seek them out and visit them without my agreement or approval was a deception and a piece of disloyalty I cannot *accept* from someone as close to me as my wife.'

Nausea bubbled in Leah's tummy. She felt sick. She felt threatened. The man she loved was lacerating her for sins she would never ever have considered committing against him. Love, not disloyalty, had driven her. Her optimism, sparked by her brother's generosity, had persuaded her to go that extra mile in the hope that a solution could be found to grant Gio a connection with his grandparents.

'Sometimes you're so stupid, Gio. You're clever about so many things but with emotions…or, apparently, possible motivations, you're hopeless. Why do you think I sneaked off to see your grandparents? What was in it for me?' Leah asked flatly. 'In reality, there was nothing in it for me except the chance of a nasty reception from your grandparents or a humiliating rejection because I was married to you. I took a risk for your benefit, not for my own. I couldn't care less about their social status. I gain nothing by you having a relationship with your grandparents—'

'So, why the hell did you do it, then?' Gio launched at her in a furious attack.

'Because I love you, and when you love someone you want them to have everything that can make them happy. You want a sunny perfect world for them and you want no bad things to happen,' Leah muttered while Gio stood staring at her, suddenly frozen to the floor by that astonishing declaration. 'That's why I did it, and I didn't tell you about what I was doing because I knew that if it went badly, it would only increase your bitterness.'

Tears sprinkling her cheeks, Leah spun and left the room to head upstairs to take refuge in the nursery. She hadn't intended to tell him how she felt about him, but it would have been worse to allow him to assume that she had decided to court his grandparents because they were titled, influential people. When misunderstandings occurred, honesty was the only solution, she reasoned wretchedly.

Unfortunately, she felt as though she had abandoned her dignity and humiliated herself because the last time she had told a man she loved him, Oliver had been the target. And Oliver had reacted as non-committally as if she had told him it was raining. How she had cringed from that memory after finding out about his affair with Celeste! She stared down into the cots where her children slumbered, peaceful and unaware of the world beyond their cosy cocoon. Slowly she backed out of the nursery again, reminding herself that the twins were the main reason she had married Gio. She had wanted them to have a father, and in that line Gio was amazing, she reminded herself doggedly.

Oh, stop kidding yourself, she urged herself impatiently. She had married him because she wanted him, because she loved him. She almost collided with the man himself on the landing but when he tried to catch her arm, she shook him off and headed straight into her bedroom, her bedroom which had steadily become *their* bedroom. Of course, what highly sexed male was likely to say no to the sex?

Gio stood in the doorway. 'I overreacted—'

'You think?' Leah parried without looking at him, stripping off the more formal outfit she had worn to visit his grandparents and ignoring him.

'I'm sorry,' he breathed stiltedly.

'Right,' Leah said tightly.

'I lost my head, my temper... I never do that. I watched my father do it too often, saw him lash out with abuse and his fists,' he admitted in a tortured undertone.

Leah breathed in deep and slow, fiercely resisting the urge to move closer and wrap her arms round him. 'You didn't use fists and you weren't abusive. You said how you felt and that was betrayed. I underestimated the level of your sensitivity...and, no, please don't tell me that you're not sensitive, because you've got triggers as we all have. You trusted me and I shocked you by doing something you see as unforgivable—'

'I don't see it that way any more,' Gio sliced in, his dark deep voice raw and rushed. 'I reacted badly because you mean more to me than anything in this world and I'm hopelessly in love with you and the thought that you could be disloyal simply devastated me.'

Leah stilled halfway into the sundress she

was putting on. That garbled surge of confession in which he barely seemed to draw breath took her so much by surprise that her tongue was glued to the roof of her mouth. Clad in floral lingerie, she turned to focus on him with wide, disconcerted dark eyes. 'Hopelessly in love with me?' she echoed in a slightly strangled voice. 'Since when?'

'For ages. But I wasn't going to tell you, wasn't going to put myself in a weak position like that again.' Gio grimaced. 'You're braver than I am. I sort of thought you'd guess and I wouldn't have to say it.'

'Idiot,' Leah pronounced, finally donning the dress she had been holding in frozen hands at her waist.

'Possibly,' Gio conceded with a slow-burning smile that tugged at the corners of his tense mouth. 'But very much *your* idiot.'

'I wasn't ready to tell you either,' Leah conceded grudgingly, and the whole time there was this surging inner joy interfering with every other thought process. He loved her back. This time she had gone out on a limb and it had paid off because Gio loved her. Every insecurity fell away, every fear was vanquished. 'But you are pretty special…in some ways,' she added, not wanting to flatter him too much.

Gio gave her a wide slanting grin. 'I suppose I could say the same thing about you. You're not quite so special when I'm tripping over the shoes you leave lying around or when you leave make-up cluttering the bathroom—'

'Don't be so *literal*!' Leah shot at him. 'You're not supposed to tell me that you love me in one breath and then in the next tell me what I do that irritates you.'

Gio's grin grew even wider as he crossed the distance separating them and tugged her into his arms. 'Clearly, I need training—'

'You do,' Leah agreed, rather covertly leaning into the heat and strength of him, still not quite accustomed to the idea of actually being loved back, accepting that she needed a little time to luxuriate in that security before she could overcome her defensiveness. Her hands slid up from his shoulders into his black hair, flirting with the tips of the silky strands. 'But you're very sexy. That comes naturally.'

Engaged in unbuttoning the straps on her shoulders, Gio glanced up with his stunning eyes semi-screened by lush ebony lashes. It was a look that made her heart skip a beat and butterflies go crazy in her tummy. 'Well, you did once give me the feeling that all you wanted from me was sex...'

Leah flushed to the roots of her hair. 'But... er—'

'You slept with me and kept on walking away again. What else was I going to think?' Gio chided. 'It was a new experience for me not to be chased. Being challenged didn't do me any harm at first, but then I saw you with Ari and assumed he was a rival and that was hell. I've never been jealous before. By the time I found Gabriella in bed with another man, the marriage and any feelings I'd had for her were dead. I'd realised I'd married someone I didn't have a thought or feeling in common with and it was a sobering experience—'

'And yet you married me—'

'By that stage I knew I didn't want a life without you or our children—'

'It was the same with me for you when I agreed to marry you. You weren't offering me love,' Leah admitted, feeling a swell of happiness rise inside her like an unstoppable tide because everything she had ever wanted with Gio was suddenly right there in front of her, 'but there was this enormous need to be with you and I couldn't resist it—'

'Why should you have been able to resist it

when I couldn't?' Gio asked, efficiently removing her last item of clothing with the single-minded resolve that was so much a part of him. When he set his heart on something he would do anything to win it and she felt so lucky that he had fallen for her. 'That's what love is...'

'Where do you think we'll be twenty years from now?' she asked him sunnily, positively buoyant with joy and optimism now that she had his heart and appreciation.

Gio laughed. 'We'll be the same. People don't change but I bet we have more kids. And in the near future I imagine I'm going to meet my grandparents...am I right?'

Leah went pink. 'I invited them to the christening.'

'Clever, enough people around to avoid each other if we don't click but the chance to connect if we do and take it further. You really are amazing,' Gio told her, pressing her down on the bed to cover her with kisses and show her all the ways in which he was also amazing.

Seven years later, in honour of their wedding anniversary, Gio and Leah and the family were in Norfolk staying at Shore House. Sally was coming to dinner with Tom, the widower who had recently become her regular companion, and Gio was cooking. It would be one of those relaxed, informal evenings that they both so much enjoyed but rarely experienced.

As she finished dressing, she glanced out of the window to check her family, who were all on the beach. They were all so active and athletic that they put her to shame. Aurora and Luca were squabbling over a ball game.

She could tell by their stances with each other, and then Aurora went to thump Luca, who always wound her up into a rage, and Gio was suddenly there, pulling the twins to him and, no doubt, once again explaining why it wasn't all right to get physical when someone annoyed you. Luca was laughing because he loved to see his sister get mad and have to deal with her frustration. Luca was far too clever for his own good. Their five-year-old, Talia, named for her great-grandmother, tugged at her father's jacket to get his attention because her siblings' argument had interrupted her seashell gathering. Their three-year-old, Rocco, was hanging onto Talia. The little boy followed Talia around like a puppy dog.

For a moment sadness shadowed Leah's eyes as she remembered Spike, who had had a very good innings, who indeed had lived to a very old age and passed away peacefully. Leah had shed many tears over his departure and Gio's surviving wolfhound had been so devastated at the loss of his only companion that they had had to replace Spike with another rescue dog, which Sally had been delighted to provide them with.

Their family was complete, both animal and child, Leah mused. But there had been losses from the family circle as well. Gio's grandfather, Eufrasio, had died two years earlier and, several months ago, Matalia, Gio's grandmother, had agreed to move into their home in Italy. She had her own annexe at the *castello* but loved being within reach of a busy household again with plenty of visitors, many of the child variety, and assistance if she needed it. Leah had never regretted going that extra mile to reunite her husband with his grandparents and over the years since he had thanked her many times for taking the risk of losing face that he himself could not bear. Gio hadn't had that long with his grandfather, but they had become close during the time they had been blessed with and Matalia, well acquainted now with Gio's kind heart and attachment to his family, adored her grandson.

And the family circle had grown and not only with children, Leah mused fondly. She had rediscovered her lost kid sister, Eloise, as well. Eloise, however, was no longer called her original birth name and the trials and tribulations that had brought her to her current status were another story entirely. Leah saw her sister as regularly as she saw her brother, Ari, and his family. Every Christmas they took turns and staged a family festive celebration and the next Christmas, it would be Leah and Gio's home that housed everyone.

Gio strolled into the bedroom and found Leah on the window seat, a favourite spot of hers where she tended to daydream. She wore a beautifully tailored casual blue top with her favourite jeans, the top outlining the swell of her breasts, the jeans showing off her shapely thighs, and that fast he wanted her again with the seething hunger that only Leah had ever inspired in him. The more time he had with her, the greedier he got, he conceded with a slanting grin.

'What are you doing?' he asked, and she turned her head, black curls bouncing on her shoulders inciting his hand to rise.

'Being lazy, watching the rest of you on the beach.' Inured to Gio's every move, Leah jerked her head out of reach of his fingers. 'No, I finally got the frizz out—'

'Only you see the frizz in your hair. I only see glossy ringlets,' Gio confided truthfully.

'I love you, but I want my hair nice for this evening.' Leah rested big caramel eyes on him, her pink mouth pouting, and it was too much for him.

'Gio!' she shrieked as he grabbed her up into his arms and kissed her breathless.

'You see, you should've let me stroke your hair. I would've been satisfied with that,' he teased her as she came back at him for another kiss.

'Liar,' she muttered against his lips.

Gio smiled down at her, his black hair tousled from the beach, his stunning eyes glittering with energy. He smelled of the sea and the outdoors and she drank in the scent of him like the addict she was, slender fingers tracing that very kissable mouth of his as she rejoiced in the reality that he was hers, all hers, as much hers as he could be. He was never off the phone when he was away from her. He took interest in every little thing that she and the kids did. She couldn't have found herself a better man and was still grateful that he hadn't given up on her, because she didn't want to think how empty her life would have been without him and the children.

'You are wearing your new pearls,' Gio finally noted with satisfaction, fingertips brushing the perfectly matched string at her throat, his gift for their anniversary to match the heavy pearl drop earrings he had given her for her last birthday. 'I want to see you in them naked in the pool at midnight to commemorate the way we met—'

Leah adored him but she rolled her eyes as if she had never heard anything so ridiculous. 'We do that every year—'

Glittering eyes intent, Gio ran the tip of his tongue across her collarbone, making her quiver with anticipation. 'I've got game to bring—'

'You've always got game to bring,' Leah murmured cheerfully, her body melting, but they both knew that their guests would be arriving soon and then there would be the fuss of the children going to bed and there just wasn't time unless they left it all to their nanny, and they only liked to do that when they had no option. They were both aware from watching some of the kids in the family circle that children grew up terrifyingly fast and they didn't want to miss out on the cuddles and the bed-time-story phase.

'Is that a fact, Signora Zanetti?' Gio teased,

hungrily assessing her with his eyes. '*Dio mio*, I love you…'

'And I love you too,' Leah told him softly, scrambling off the bed before she gave way to temptation, which was so easy with Gio. 'Until midnight…'

* * * * *

If you couldn't put
The Heirs His Housekeeper Carried *down,*
you're sure to love the first instalment in
The Stefanos Legacy trilogy
Promoted to the Greek's Wife

Don't miss the final instalment,
coming soon!

In the meantime, why not get lost in these
other stories by Lynne Graham?

Christmas Babies for the Italian
The Greek's Convenient Cinderella
The Ring the Spaniard Gave Her
Cinderella's Desert Baby Bombshell
Her Best Kept Royal Secret

Available now!